Of Thorns and Roses

Of Thorns and Roses

Asma Zehra

PARTRIDGE
A Penguin Random House Company

To order additional copies of this book, contact
Partridge India
000 800 10062 62
www.partridgepublishing.com/india
orders.india@partridgepublishing.com

CONTENTS

ACKNOWLEDGEMENT

I would like to express my greatest gratitute to my son, Aman not only for his support and encouragement, but also for his patience, inputs and belief in my work.

Of Thorns and Roses

PROLOGUE

Tears rolled down her cheek as her heart beat faster and faster. It throbbed so loudly that she could hear it clearly despite all the commotion. She stood up. She felt as if it was all a movie scene, unravelling in slow motion. The volcano erupted and lava flowed. Each step trying to pull her back; each step taking her away from herself. She turned around to look at the frail, motionless figure of her six-year-old son, Keith. Her eyes blurred with warm tears that flowed down her face. She tried hard to stop, but found herself rushing to embrace his fragile body tightly. She did not want to let go, but knew she had to. There was no choice. It was a race against time and she *had* to win. She looked at her mobile phone helplessly, wishing it would ring, just once, but it did not.

Vidya, the ever-so-confident, bubbly, vibrant and successful 34-year-old vice president of a media house, felt like she was somebody else, somebody completely unlike herself, at the moment. She had been at the Kishen Seth Hospital's casualty for the past hour. Ambulance sirens screamed continuously as more and more people flowed into the already flooded hospital.

The atmosphere was chaotic and desperate, filled with cries and mourning. She had never seen so much blood in her life, though the pain of death was not new to her. She shook her head resolutely, refusing to let memories of another day so like this sweep her away in its tide. She stared at the middle-aged man screaming in pain, holding on to his ripped arm, as another was brought in with an oozing eye. There was one whose scalp was ripped open. It was a gory sight.

Vidya was numb to all the pain that was all around her, oblivious to the surroundings. All she could think of was Keith. But was she really thinking? No, she was scared. Scared? Was that the right word? She felt the same helplessness wash over her once again; the feeling she had hated all her life. The one she thought she had escaped, the feeling that had kept her awake all those cold, dark nights.

"Lord! Why me? Why me again?" she kept murmuring, her eyes turning up as if expecting an answer from above, only to see the dull ceiling covered with cobwebs.

"Sister! Please . . . Please . . . Please," she pleaded once again, trying to stop the nurse rushing into the Operation Theatre. Her voice choked and her words were barely audible over the groans and cries that filled the air.

"Sorry madam," was all that the nurse could say as she hurried on holding bags of blood, pulling the door closed after her with a click that seemed final to Vidya.

She lifted her eyes once again to see the face of the *paan*-chewing, bald attendant dressed all in white. His smile seemed to mock her misery. She felt like scraping those insolent eyes off his face. As though reading her thoughts, he gestured towards Keith and she turned once again to look at her son who lay in a corner on the floor. She was scared the rush of doctors and nurses would trample him underfoot.

Vidya had to make a decision, and she had to make it now. She nodded to the attendant and his lips parted in a vile smile that showed stained and yellow teeth.

She felt she'd puke as she walked towards the gruesome attendant. She wished in vain that time would stand still.

She froze as a sudden realization hit her—a realization that had come so late in life. Wails, louder than all the others, echoed in the crowded room and she was dimly surprised to notice they were her own. Her cries got louder, tearing through her soul and her very existence.

CHAPTER 1

The Moving Lanterns

It would be another hour before the sun's rays could tear through the darkness to reach earth. She could hear the bucket hitting the walls of the well and water falling back into the dark pit – so Nana and Amma were already up. That had to be Nana. He always bathed Gauri and Laxmi before he milked them. The swish of the broom told her that Amma was already sweeping the veranda. She would then sprinkle water and draw a beautiful *rangoli*, as she did every morning.

Vidya, lying on the mat in her tiny hut, turned over and pulled the sheet over her head. She curled up to go back to sleep. She still had some time before the train would chug along, when she would run out and wave to the passengers. She snuggled back under the sheet as Gauri called out, "*Ambaaaaaaaa*".

"Hush! Softly Gauri, Vidya's still sleeping," she could hear Nana admonishing before settling down with the buckets.

She could smell the coal smoulder and the tea boil. A few more minutes, she thought to herself before dozing off once again.

"Koooooooooooooooooooo!" and little Vidya jumped up, racing into the open. "Slowly dear, you may fall," Nana called after her, but did Vidya ever listen? Her tiny feet raced towards the fence. Dawn hadn't quite broken and a few stars could still be seen in the receding dark, but she knew her courtyard well. She waved mightily, jumping with joy as the red serpent wound its way through the fog and the dew. She could see the engine driver, the different coaches and the passengers. A few windows were shut, some open with dim lights that seemed like moving lanterns. A few passengers peeped out as though looking at her.

"Taaataaaaaa, taaataaaa!" Her voice was full of joy as one odd passenger waved back at her.

Aah! What a wonderful morning! The cool breeze kissed her pretty face and ruffled her long, silky hair. As the train crawled out of sight, Vidya ran back to embrace her father. "Nana, Nana," she called, and was up in his strong arms in a second.

There was a smile of joy on Vidya's face as he gently kissed her forehead before throwing her up into the air only to catch her in a moment. Vidya's laughter rung out clear as glass, as the early sparrows chirped in the background. Amma came with a big glass of steaming hot tea held by her *pallu*. Vidya jumped out of Nana's arms only to run and cling to Amma.

"Careful, dear," Amma said softly, handing the tea to Nana, and then bending to kiss her before holding her tiny arm and leading her away.

"I want to see those pearls white and bright," Nana said aloud as he did each morning.

"Eeee," Vidya said as she turned to show her teeth before going inside with Amma.

"Thaatha, I will also come with you," she called to her grandfather, who was ready with the milk cans on his *Atlas* cycle.

"Not before you finish your glass of milk," said Amma as they hurried towards the *baawdi*, where an aluminium bucket full of water was waiting for Vidya.

Amma struggled to scrub her teeth with the black **manjan**, holding Vidya with one hand. Vidya giggled as the cold water splashed on her face. She pulled Amma's pallu to wipe herself and was off racing towards the cycle under the lush mango tree, when Amma called out, "Vidya, your milk, dear."

"Give it to me," said Nana as Vidya tried to hide behind her Thaatha's white **dhoti**.

"Honey, drink fast or we will miss the van," said Thaatha as Nana bent down with the copper glass, smiling at her.

She gulped down the milk with a smirk on her face. Thaatha lifted little Vidya up and settled her on the handlebar before sitting on the dull blue seat. Soon, they were peddling away down the muddy track which looked more like a game trail made by the footsteps of the few who came down to their humble dwelling.

Vidya loved the ride on the bicycle, especially when she could ring its big steel bell. *Trrrrrrrriii iiinggggggggg . . . trrrrrrrrriiiiiinggggggggg . . . . trrrrrrrrriiiiiinggggggggg*! She announced their way as they passed the lush green paddy fields. It was an old cycle, a little rusty, with big wheels and tyres that had almost worn through. It squeaked as Thaatha peddled along the way. Early birds' songs filled the air as a white **sarus** flew past. When they neared the lake, Vidya could see a **neelkanth** perched on a branch with a few ducks swimming in the silvery waters on which pink water lilies floated prettily.

It was going to be a beautiful day. Thaatha peddled briskly to reach the highway where a big lorry was parked under the peepal. Stopping near the gathering, Thaatha helped Vidya off the cycle before he got down.

"Aah! Here comes Ramulu with Vidya. Sweetie, how are you today?" Saianna called out as he came and lifted Vidya up in his arms.

Vidya returned the warm smile as Thaatha got the milk measured before taking out a small book and making a note of it.

Vidya wriggled out of Saianna's arms and ran across to catch a lamb as a herd of sheep crossed the road. Thaatha squatted down to share a *beedi* with his friends as they huddled together to catch a few minutes with each other, a daily ritual.

"Vidya, come dear, time to go back," called Thaatha, throwing away the beedi stub and getting back on his Atlas. Vidya ran to Thaatha, who picked her up to gently put her back on the handlebar, and they were off back home.

CHAPTER 2

Dreams Of A Beautiful Bride

By the time they got home, clothes were dripping on the clothesline, a simple rope held up by bamboo sticks. Amma was scrubbing Nana's back near the well and the aroma of hot rice filled the air as it boiled in the earthen pot. The golden bells tinkled on the necks of Laxmi, Gauri and Bheema.

Bheema was white, big and strong. Nana had painted his horns red, which made him look more robust. He had gentle eyes and the strength of ten bison. He swished his long tail every now and then. His golden bell was bigger than Gauri's or Laxmi's, who were auburn and looked more demure.

"They are sisters," Amma had told Vidya once. Their mother was Sita, who had died a few years ago during the draught. Bheema had been bought at the yearly cow *mela* much before Vidya was born.

It was not a new story, but Vidya loved it so much that she used to ask Nana to narrate it 'one more time' so many times. Nana had a knack for storytelling. He made things sound so dramatic yet so real.

"It so happened," Nana would start in his masculine yet surprisingly gentle voice, "that your Amma and I had gone to your aunt's wedding. It was a long journey. It had not rained enough that year, and there wasn't much to do in the fields. Besides, your Amma had been planning for her sister's wedding for a long time. It was one of those few occasions where she got to wear her red silk saree, the one she looked so lovely in on our wedding day. The red silk saree with a big golden border. You know your Amma looks like a fairy when she wears that saree and puts those jasmine flowers in her hair after she ties in a big bun."

"Nana, when will you get me a red silk saree with a golden border just like Amma's?" Vidya would interrupt to ask Nana as Amma shyly looked up with a coy smile on her lips.

"On your wedding darling! I will buy you the best silk saree. Better than Amma's," Nana would say lovingly.

"And also *jhumkas* and bangles".

"Of course, dear. You will be the most beautiful bride."

"And who will be my groom?"

"He will be a prince from a land far away. He will come wearing a nice suit and a big hat, in a big, white motorcar to take your hand and drive away with you into the world of dreams."

Vidya would laugh aloud and clap her tiny hands with joy. The thought of dressing up as a bride in rich new clothes with bangles and jewels excited her.

She would lose track of Bheema's story for a while and start dreaming of being the beautiful bride Nana described. She too would look like her mother with her long hair neatly plaited with *mogra* flowers wrapped down its length. She would wear *kajal* to be a doe-eyed beauty. She would blush on seeing her groom from the corner of her eye. Oh! It sounded like a fairy tale.

"Enough of that," Amma would say as she chopped fresh okras with the *draanti*, bringing father and daughter back to Bheema's story.

"So, where was I?" Nana would ask.

"Amma looking from the corner of her eyes in the silk saree," Vidya would reply instantly.

"No," Amma would interrupt. "We were going to my sister's wedding along with Sita."

"Aah. Sita," Nana would continue. "She was very beautiful. She was blackish-brown with a white crescent shaped moon on her forehead. I used to milk her every day like Gauri and Laxmi. We would then go to plough the fields but as it was a dry season that year, we got the cart and set out on that long journey. Your Amma made a few *jowar rotis* for the way." Vidya would move closer to sit on Nana's lap as he held her gently.

"It took us two days by the cart. We stopped by the big yellow sunflower fields. The flowers were so big that one flower was enough to cover Amma's big bun."

"Oooh!" Vidya would say aloud as Nana described the journey.

"There was this beautiful pond where we rested for some time under a big tamarind tree to have lunch before setting off once again." Vidya would be all ears as the story continued.

"We had to cross the jungle before dusk and get to the highway to reach the nearest village where we rested for the night in a *dharmshala*."

"Are there big tigers in the jungle Nana?" Vidya would ask enthusiastically.

"Big and ferocious."

"Were you not scared?" Vidya would ask, wide-eyed as she clenched Nana's hand tightly.

"Of course not! I would have punched the tiger in his face with my fist and it would have run away with a bloody nose."

Vidya would exclaim loudly. She believed every word her father uttered. He was so big and strong. He could definitely scare any beast away.

"The wedding was a grand affair," Nana would continue. "The food was scrumptious and we ate till we were full."

"What all did you eat?"

"Oh, there were *vadas, idlis* and *dosas* with coconut *chutney* and piping hot *sambhar* for breakfast, and then there was rice, *pappu, maavdikaai pachchidi, papads,* fresh vegetable curry, *perugu, pongal, rasam, nai, vadiaalu* and so much more before we were served *paal paayasam.*" Vidya's mouth would water at this part. She loved food.

"Will you make all those for my wedding?" she would ask.

"Of course, dear!" Nana would assure her before continuing the story.

"The day after the wedding, I went to the annual animal fair where hundreds of cows, buffaloes and bulls were brought to be sold. Their owners wore big colourful turbans and had bigger moustaches. They looked as impressive and strong as their cattle. There were bull fights and races. The cattle were well bathed and decorated with big bells, painted horns. A few even had garlands on their necks. There was heavy bidding throughout the three days of the sale. Prospective buyers flocked to check the cows before moving ahead to bid on the one they found the most impressive, bargaining hard. The cattle sellers told tales about the bravery and strength of the bulls, how much milk the cows gave every day; they said everything to lure customers and get the best offer. There was such a big crowd and such commotion all around that dry, dusty summer afternoon.

We sweated like pigs, but it was fun as it was an all-men affair." Nana's voice sounded nostalgic.

"As I went around laughing and joking with Ramanna—that's your mother's brother, you remember him—I saw an old man with a calf sitting under a barren tree. He had a big stick in his frail hand and a white turban on his head. His back was hunched with age. He struggled to get up when he saw us walking his way. We could sense his anxiousness as he looked towards us with his faded eyes." Nana's voice would change now.

"'This calf is a good breed,' the old man struggled to say in his feeble voice, trying to sound as enthusiastic as his age and health would permit. 'It will grow up to be strong and handsome,' he continued, gesturing towards the white calf tied to the tree.

'I won't charge you much.' He stopped to take a breath.

'Sorry, we have not come here to buy cattle,' said Ramanna, moving ahead.

'Why don't you go to the main ground where the bargaining is going on,' I suggested gently.

'I will get trampled,' said the old man, his voice almost choking.

'Is there no one with you who can help you?' I was genuinely concerned.

'I have this calf, which I have come to sell.'

'But why?'

'Its mother died of an infection. I used to lend her, for a little money, to the villagers who wanted to go to the big bazaars, but now that she's no more, there is no money. This poor thing will die because I cannot feed it.' The pain in his voice was evident as tears shone in his eyes. 'God will bless you if you save its life.' The old man looked at us pleadingly.

"I looked at the playful calf tied with a small rope to the tree. It looked back at me with its big black mischievous eyes.

'I will spread the word around,' I said, trying to move ahead as the old man sat down again wiping his sweat with his turban.

"I patted the calf lovingly and moved on to catch up with Ramanna. I'd moved a few feet away when I heard the calf go 'Maaaa'. The old man shouted faintly. 'Stop, stop . . . . Stop, you rogue . . . Wait.'

"Angered by the words, I turned around to see the little angel running towards me. It had managed to break loose. It still had a part of the rope tied around its neck. I bent down to hold it as it stopped near me. It started jumping as if playing with me. I patted it once again and was mesmerised by its playful, innocent eyes.

'How much for him, Thaatha?' I asked the old man with a wrinkled face as he got near me, panting and gasping loudly.

'What?' He did not understand.

'How much for this little devil?'

"And that is how Bheema became a part of our family."

Vidya would always fall asleep before Nana narrated how he had to face Amma's temper when he got back with Bheema instead of the saree and bangles he had promised her.

The trio were the pride of Vidya's family and they looked beautiful together.

After a quick wash, they went out walking barefoot towards their field to start the day as the sun rose in the crimson sky above.

Amma carried food in a bamboo basket which she placed on her head while Nana and Thaatha walked along with Laxmi, Gauri and Bheema. Little Vidya ran ahead, running, jumping, stopping for a moment to turn back and check if she'd gone too far ahead before running ahead again. When she got a bit tired, Nana would put her on Bheema's back and she would sit on it as a princess would on an elephant howdah.

CHAPTER 3

Love That Never Crossed The River

At the confluence of two rivers and surrounded by mist-shrouded hills nestled the lush fertile plains of the hamlet and large forest areas. During spring, blooms covered the hillsides in bursts of colour, with herbs forming their own patches of different shades of green. The village was beautiful and peaceful. Every year, thousands of birds flocked to the crystal clear waters sweet as nectar. People, as simple as their woven attire, had their own rituals and customs. The village was like an extended family—everybody knew each other, with all involved in major decisions and petty fights resolved by the village elders.

The river, called *Devi*, was so wide and deep that fishermen set sail only on clear, sunny days. It was believed that she brought bountiful harvest and prosperity. Farmers worshipped Devi as guardian and protector. Children loved to swim in the river's cool waters while women folk washed clothes, keeping a watchful eye on the naughty bunch.

There was a saying that Devi cared for the villagers as her children, but if one sinned, they all had to bear her anger. In fury, she would swell and overflow, flooding the village.

"It so happened," the elders would say, "that decades ago, there lived a cobbler named Krishnudu in a village close by. He was tall, handsome and hardworking. He made the finest *chappals* in the whole district. His craftsmanship was such that people came from far and wide to by his wares. Krishnudu would go from one village to the next, making colourful chappals for men, women and kids.

"One day, he happened to come to this village by the river. He met Rukumani, the lovely daughter of Ramaswamy, the head priest of the temple. They fell in love and would meet under a big banyan tree.

"Soon, the villagers came to know of their story. The priest and the *pujaris* were flabbergasted. 'How can a priest's daughter love a lowly cobbler, who makes chappals for a living?' questioned the custodians of faith.

"They caught hold of Krishnudu and beat him to a pulp. He was produced before the Panchayat. The whole village assembled to witness the proceedings. He had committed a grave offence. There was silence as men and women sat on the ground while the village elders talked the matter over.

"There was a lot of discussion. Krishnudu was also given a chance to speak. It was decided that Rukumani would be married off to Pundit Ramachary's son within a fortnight. Krishnudu was ordered to stay away from the village until after the wedding. The lovers' pleas fell on deaf ears and Rukumani was escorted away under watchful eyes of the village elders and pujaris.

"Her heart broken, with nobody who could understand her, Rukumani gave up food and wept her heart out for the gods to hear.

'O Lord, why did you give me a heart and then fill it with love only for it to be broken this way?' she wailed.

"Krishnudu tried to get news of his beloved, but all in vain.

"People stopped speaking to him and would whisper in hushed voices as he passed by. His family was furious.

'How dare you do such a thing?'

'Don't you know your caste? Don't you know your place?'

'Now who will marry your sisters?'

"Questions came from every direction, but Krishnudu had no answers. He had not planned to fall in love. It just happened, but it made no sense to anyone but him – and his love. Dejected and depressed, he roamed aimlessly in the fields, on the banks and in the forest. He lovingly touched the banyan tree under which he and Rukumani often met. They had spent hours and hours together weaving dreams of their life together, all of which were now shattered. "Monsoon came and the skies opened, the rain torrential as if the skies and the clouds wept with them. Krishnudu knew well that death would be the verdict if he tried to meet Rukumani or disrupt the marriage ceremony.

"The black clouds above reminded him of Rukumani's dense tresses, which when let loose would cover her beautiful face as the cool breeze blew. He would say, 'It looks as though the clouds are covering the moon to make it look more beautiful.'

"Rukumani would blush and cover her face with her half-saree pallu. She would then raise her eyes dramatically to look at him and he would add, 'Your coy looks will kill me one day.'

"Rukumani would cover his lips with her palm. 'Hush. We have a life to live together. Never ever speak of death again.'

"Tears would choke her voice and fill her dark doe eyes. Krishnudu would struggle to make her smile again.

"The crash of thunder brought back Krishnudu to reality. He wept silently, barely noticing the rain that drenched him. He hugged the banyan tree as he would have hugged Rukumani. He knew well that his love was also in pain, and he could do nothing to ease it.

"Weddings in the village were big affairs. A wedding between two affluent priest families was even grander as villagers gathered for the festivities.

"Fresh vegetables from the fields were brought by bullock carts as were carts full of plantains. Women got together to pound fresh spices as the cooks settled down to chop the greens and pumpkins. Mangoes and coconuts in large bamboo baskets were unloaded in the pouring rain.

"Feet froze on the temple steps as the pundit shouted, 'Quick, quick!' before rushing past.

"There was a silent prayer on trembling lips. 'O Lord! Forgive me. O Lord! Help me!' Krishnudu whispered as he put down a loaded basket and silently slipped inside, unnoticed. He held his breath, trembling, but he was resolute. His heart seemed louder to him than the thunder crashing in the skies.

"As a member of a lower caste, Krishnudu had never entered the temple before and was unfamiliar with the layout. It was huge and beautiful from the outside. He had heard the bells ring during *aarti*. He loved the fragrance of the *agarbattis* as he sat below the peepal outside the temple every Friday evening, hoping to sell a few chappals.

"He had blindly followed the men carrying goods. If he were caught, if he had to run, he didn't know if or how he could escape. He shivered, but he pictured Rukumani in his mind. Her face seemed to bring him courage as he sat down in the darkest of the corners, waiting for the right time. He did not know what he could do, but he had to do something. He could not give up so easily. He told himself that the odds were against him and prepared himself for the inevitable consequences.

"As a daughter of the head priest, Rukumani lived in the temple premise, as her ancestors had. She had told him so much about the beautiful deity adorned with silk robes and ornaments; the intricate stone carvings on the walls depicting mythological stories; the sanctum-sanctorum; the elaborate pujas and aartis; the ringing of bells every morning; and the festive food and *prasad* prepared in pure *ghee* on *Diwali, Dusshera and Ganesh Chathurthi.* She'd spoken of the big banyan tree which was more than 400 years old and how women would tie colourful threads as they circled it with folded hands. Krishnudu had heard it all and had wished that he could one day go in and offer prayers, though he knew that would never happen.

"And now, here he was in one of the temple rooms hiding behind bags of rice meant for the impending wedding feast!

"Gathering courage he peeped from behind the half-shut door as *shanks* were blown and bells rang. The *Gotras* and *Nakshatras* matched perfectly. There were big smiles on everybody's faces, and the atmosphere was bright and cheerful.

'Bring the bride for the puja,' an elderly lady said aloud as Krishnudu's heart skipped a beat.

"Surrounded by women in colourful silk sarees, Rukumani walked in slowly with her head bowed. She looked like a peacock, draped in blue silk, her long hair left loose and flowing. As she raised her head a bit, Krishnudu could see her red, swollen eyes. His heart ached. Rukumani had been weeping. Never had he seen her so sad before.

"Taking a deep breath, Krishnudu muttered to himself, 'Hold on dear, I'm coming,' as he leaned his bare body against the cold wall. He peeped again to see Rukumani being led back to the room from where she was brought. It was on the other side of the courtyard.

"With the devotees dispersing, Krishnudu had his first glimpse of the Goddess. She was indeed as beautiful and divine as Rukumani had described. He could sense her power, but could not gather courage to look her in the eye. He folded his hands and prayed silently as the sanctum closed for the day.

"It must have been past midnight when all was still and Krishnudu felt it was safe. He slowly opened the door and stepped out. As the rain poured, he moved cautiously, ducking behind a pillar and glancing around before racing towards the door behind which Rukumani was held captive.

"He pushed the door cautiously, but it was latched from within. It was an old timber door with a few cracks through which he could see a flickering lamp. Rukumani sat on the floor, her knees drawn up, head bowed and resting on them. There were two elderly ladies fast asleep beside her.

"Krishnudu tried to push the door again. It creaked and he froze as one woman shifted. Rukumani sat there as if lost in a dream, oblivious to the world.

"The space between the doors was not large enough to slide his fingers through and open the latch. Krishnudu had to do something fast. He looked around searching for something. He then moved like lightning towards the peepal tree in the courtyard and picked up part of a broken branch before rushing back.

"The pitter patter of rain drops drowned out his footsteps. He was cold with fear and his hands shook. Taking a deep breath, he pushed the stick through the crack, trying to unlatch the door. *Tak!* There was a crack and the stick broke. Rukumani lift her face for the first time as part of the stick fell inside the room. She barely seemed able to make out what was happening. After what seemed like an eternity, she slowly rose and moved to open the door.

"The tinkle of her anklets woke the lady, who saw Krishnudu and shrieked. There was no time to lose. Grabbing hold of Rukumani's hand, he asked, 'Which way?' and they ran together towards the door. As they scrambled up the steps, they could hear shouts; heavy footsteps followed.

"Krishnudu turned back to see dozens of people with *lathis* and knives rushing at them. The tranquil of the night was filled screams: 'Stop! Stop, you scoundrel. Stop or we will kill you both.'

"Krishnudu held Rukumani's hand tighter as they sprinted through the fields and towards the river. He had a boat ready there. They would cross the river and go to the big city of which he had heard, where they would lose themselves in the crowd and live happily ever after. He had it all planned in his mind. He would make lovely chappals there and would soon settle down. As they reached the bank, he pushed Rukumani into the boat before untying it, pushing off into the river and jumping in. He rowed the boat with all his might as rain splashed heavily. The waves were so high that he struggled to keep the boat balanced.

"Looking back after a while, he took a deep breath. He could see the crowd throwing sticks and knives at them, still shouting in the dark with *mashals* in their hands. He did not worry now. They were a safe distance away and their shouts were fading, drowned out by the splashing of the oars and the rain.

"For the first time after the frantic escape, Krishnudu looked at Rukumani. She was still gasping for breath and pale with fear. He moved forward to take her in his strong arms.

"It rained heavily that night as clouds seemed to burst. Lightning streaked the sky over and over again. Thunder roared in anger.

"The next morning, the remains of the broken boat were found in the neighbouring village. The lovers were never found—dead or alive.

"The priest proclaimed, 'Devi has judged and punished,' as the temple was cleansed with holy water and prayers offered."

CHAPTER 4

Before Diwali

Vidya loved going to the Sunday Bazaar held in the Ramleela ground. This was one day the whole village looked forward to as vendors from all the 20 villages around came to sell their goods.

There were sarees of vibrant colours, bangles to match, fancy chappals, cloth for shirts and trousers for men, toys and balloons for kids and more. Potters would bring clay pots. There were knives *daraantis*, sickles and *sabbals*. There were *bandis* where hot *bajjis* and *vadas* were sold as another hawker prepared fresh and juicy *jalebis*. Ice *golas* and *kulfis* sold like hot cakes, as did the colourful juices. Sugarcane juice with a dash of ginger was indeed refreshing in the hot summer afternoon. Vidya loved the colourful *bindis* and bangles.

Vidya accompanied her father to the bazaar and had lots of fun on the wooden cartwheel pushed by the *jhulawaala*. "Nana . . . Nana," Vidya would call out from the top and wave.

Nana had bought a portable radio from the bazaar and now the afternoons were filled with songs from the movies. Vidya would dance merrily in the fields. Nana would also tune in to listen to the news from the big cities and the weather forecast, which Vidya could never understand.

It was a 20-minute walk to the field. It wasn't a very big one, but enough to feed the family. Crops were grown in rotation. It would be okras one season, and tomatoes another, then cluster beans and brinjals. They did not grow rice because that cost too much money. Amma and Nana would toil the whole day as Thaatha would hitch the cart to Laxmi and Gouri and take people from one village to another. He would also take vegetables to the market along with Nana and sell them to the *thekedar*.

"I will miss you next season," Nana told Amma sadly.

"I will stay if you want me to," Amma replied.

"No, you have to go. You need rest. Don't worry about me. I'll be fine."

"Where is Amma going?" asked a worried Vidya.

"She is going to your grandmother's place," replied Nana. "Your uncle is coming next week to take you both."

"But why?"

"You see," Nana explained in a tender loving voice, "your Amma is going to bring you a small brother, who will play with you. For that, you and Amma have to go to your grandmother's place."

Vidya was excited. "A baby brother?"

"Yes. A tiny little baby brother for Vidya."

"But why do we have to go alone? Why can't you come?"

"I have work in the fields and besides, who will look after Laxmi, Gauri and Bheema?"

"Yes, that's right," said Vidya, her voice low. "I will miss you Nana," she said.

"I will come to see you, darling!" Nana reassured.

"When is my brother coming?"

"Before Diwali, before your birthday."

"That means we can burst crackers together!" exclaimed Vidya as Nana laughed.

Sai was born a healthy baby. Vidya loved her little brother. He was so small; Vidya was fascinated with how tiny he was, especially his soft feet and hands. She would sit beside Amma and try to help change the cloth nappies. She would want to hold him and Amma would make her sit beside her and place Sai on her little lap, still holding on to him. Vidya would lovingly touch his forehead and plant kisses on his little cheeks. "I am now a big sister," she would say proudly.

Days passed and Nana came down to take them back. Vidya woke up early that morning to greet her father. She was so happy.

CHAPTER 5

Keith

"Vidya . . . . Who is Vidya," called out a voice loudly.

Vidya was startled. "It's me, it's me," she cried.

"Call for you," called out the lady at the reception as she struggled with the crowd at her desk and the ringing phones.

Vidya rushed to pick the phone.

"Hello!" She said in an anxious voice. She was relieved to hear Bill's voice at the other end.

"How's Keith?" Bill sounded worried.

"He's not fine. He's not fine at all," sobbed Vidya. "All the doctors are busy and there are no free operation theatres. There is no one to take care of Keith. He hasn't opened his eyes. He is bleeding . . . ." her voice broke.

Had she been in London, she would have called 911 and made sure that Keith was airlifted to the nearest hospital, where doctors and nurses would ensure the best of medical care. But here she was in a small village, where basic necessities were so lacking.

"Hold on," said Bill, reassuring her. "I'm on my way. I'll get there soon. I have made all arrangements. We will take Keith to the city. He will be fine."

"Come soon, please, come soon!" is all that Vidya could say before the lady at the reception curtly asked her to cut her conversation short.

Vidya felt miserable. She rushed towards Keith and hugged him. She kissed his forehead.

"Wake up, darling! Open your eyes! It's me. Mom!" her voice broke as she sobbed.

A hand touched her shoulder and she looked up angrily, but it was Bill. He picked up Keith and rushed out, with Vidya following at a run. "Come on, hurry."

They raced towards the waiting car. "It's an hour's drive to the city," he said as he put Keith on the back seat.

"This is Dr. Morgan," he hurriedly introduced an elderly man in the car whom Vidya had barely noticed. For once, there was no time for courtesies. Vidya jumped in the car and Bill hurried into the driver's seat, starting the car without taking the time to settle in.

"Doctor, please do something," Vidya pleaded.

"Please let me check. I want you to be patient and let me work." Dr. Morgan got straight on the job checking Keith's pulse and giving him an injection.

Dr. Morgan then went on to clean Keith's wound and bandage him up. He struggled in the limited space as Bill floored the pedal on the highway.

Vidya saw a ray of hope at last. "Drive faster, faster!" she insisted.

"Bill, stop the car and let the lady out," said Dr. Morgan in a stern voice. "I cannot treat the patient under such pressure."

Vidya felt helpless as she fell silent. She kept turning to look at Keith as Dr. Morgan successfully inserted the intravenous syringe in his wrist, stuck in securely and held up the bottle filled with clear fluid.

"Don't worry," he said, his voice assuring for the first time. "I have given him an injection and this saline will supplement his body until we reach the city hospital. Keith's situation is grave, but not hopeless. He has lost a lot of blood, but I am quite sure he will be fine. He is unconscious, but his pulse not too weak."

The comforting words meant a lot to Vidya. She took a deep breath. At last someone was speaking of Keith in a positive light, and that someone was a *doctor*. He would know.

She looked at Bill as he patted her hand for a second.

"You need to calm down," said Bill as he steered.

Vidya nodded, but she knew she could not relax until Keith opened his eyes and spoke to her.

"Baby, you'll be fine," she murmured to Keith. "I'll get you your favourite Superman costume. I promise." Her voice trailed off as they reached the hospital, screeching to a halt in front of the ER.

Nurses rushed to place Keith on the stretcher and push it as Dr. Morgan and Bill tried to keep pace. Vidya held on to Keith's hand, only letting go of it as he was rushed into the operation theatre. The big door closed and the red light above it turned on.

There was a sense of relief now as the nurse rushed in with bottles of blood. This time, the blood was for Keith. Vidya cried again. Her tears were now of hope as she prayed silently, holding Bill's hand, as he drew her close and hugged her tight. She cried on his shoulder and he let her cry, patting her head gently.

CHAPTER 6

Conflicting Ideas

Vidya was enrolled in the local village school. Thaatha would drop her on his *Atlas* cycle in the morning and pick her up in the evening.

The village school was an old, thatched structure with five classrooms. Often, classes were held in the open, under trees. Vidya loved going to school as she made new friends. She was fond of reading and loved the stories that her teachers taught her. She would come back and chatter excitedly about her day to Amma and Nana as she played with Sai.

"You know Nana," she would say, "There are so many other fruits apart from mangoes and bananas. My teacher showed me photos in the book." She would then take out her alphabet book and show the pictures. "See, this is an apple, and this is a pineapple, and this one," she would go on, turning the pages, "is called a pear."

Earlier, Nana used to tell Vidya stories. But now it was her turn; she shared stories she had heard at school, dozing off half way through.

"I am going to make my daughter a big doctor," Nana would tell Amma.

"Stop day-dreaming," Amma would try to cut him short. "Our village school has classes only up to the 5th standard, and besides, who educates the girls so much? How can Vidya become a doctor?"

"We will go to the city. There are big schools there."

"And what about the fields? Do you know how much money it takes to make a living in the city? My cousin stays in the city and she told me how difficult it is. You hardly find work."

"I will toil day and night. I have named her Vidya. I will get her educated," Nana would emphasise.

"Alright, we'll see that later. Here, have food first." Amma was an expert in changing the subject.

She had heard stories of the big bad city. She did not think it would be a good idea to leave the comfort and security of the village and the fields to struggle in the unknown cities. Vidya had to be married off, she reasoned. There was no educated girl in the whole village and she did not see any way there could be one. She wanted to stay grounded, wiser and more rational, but Nana thought otherwise.

CHAPTER 7

Rakshasa and The Amavasya Moon

Vidya threw her black slate onto the *charpoi* as she sat down with a glum face.

"What's the matter darling? Why isn't my mynah chirping today?" asked Nana wiping his hands with an old towel as he walked towards Vidya. This was so unlike her. She always ran into his arms when she saw him.

"What's your name Nana?" asked Vidya in a cross voice.

"Venkatlu."

"And why did you not tell me before?"

"Why? What happened darling?"

"My teacher asked me your name today and I did not know it." Her voice was muffled.

"Sorry darling."

"You know how my friends laughed at me?" she was about to cry.

That night as Vidya and her father lay on the charpoi in the veranda as they usually did after dinner, looking at the stars in the clear summer night, music playing softly on the radio.

"You see those tiny stars above?"

"Yes Nana, they are sooooo beautiful and I love the moon."

"They are far away," Nana continued looking upwards as a bat flew by, "yet they shine so brightly and can be seen throughout the world."

"Yes, Nana," Vidya nodded. "Isn't it amazing?"

"You know love, whenever I see you, I see a spark; a spark that can light up the world."

"Like the moon?"

"Yes, like the moon."

"But where is it?" asked Vidya innocently looking at herself.

"It is within you, waiting to glow like the moon."

"But I don't want to be like the moon."

"Why not?"

"The *Rakshasa* eats it up one bite a night and then it is gobbled up every *Amavas*."

Nana laughed aloud. "Who told you so?" he asked.

"Amma told me everything" replied Vidya.

Turning towards Vidya, who was looking at him keenly, Nana took a deep breath. "Vidya," he said, "nature reveals the truth of life if you have the time to look carefully."

"Like what?" asked Vidya eagerly.

"Like the moon."

"Like the moon?"

"Yes. Like the moon." Nana explained further. "Our lives are filled with struggles, pains, worries, which trouble us day-in and day-out; but if you develop strength and determination like the moon, we can fight the *Rakshasa* to become *Poonam* once again."

"There are thousands of stars," Nana continued, "but only one moon, which outshines them all."

Vidya snuggled closer to her father, sure that he was the wisest man who ever lived.

Although Vidya was young, Nana's words would have a lasting impact on her, to guide her throughout her life.

CHAPTER 8

Sai

Nana had tied a saree to a branch of the now flowering mango tree to make Sai's cradle. Amma would place Sai in it when she went about doing the chores, while Vidya would gently rock the baby to sleep.

"Vidya is turning out to be very sensible and mature," the neighbouring ladies noticed. Amma smiled with pride at Vidya, who would sometimes try to sweep the veranda with her tiny hands as Amma nursed Sai. Amma would not keep Vidya from doing small tasks. She believed that girls should learn housework as that was what they had to do when they grew up. Nana would object at times, but Amma reasoned with him.

"I am not forcing her. She enjoys it," she would say. "Let her learn the fun way. It will be useful for her in the future."

Nana would grumble and move away.

Soon Sai started crawling and Vidya would happily keep an eye on him, playing hop-scotch with Chinni, her neighbour. She loved Sai dearly.

"Look Sai, this is Laxmi and this is Gauri," she would tell him, pointing at the cows. "They give milk. When you grow up, you too can have a glass every morning. In fact you can have mine too. It will make you strong like Nana," she said.

Thaatha laughed "Trying to get rid of your share, are you?"

"Hush, Thaatha, not so loud! Amma will hear and I will be caught," said Vidya in a hushed tone.

"Okay, okay." Thaatha moved away, still smiling as the train whistled and Vidya ran to wave at it.

"Sai, this is a train. See, so long and beautiful," she shouted as the train chugged lazily along the tracks. "When you grow up, we will both wave at it together. It is so much fun!" Vidya's voice was full of excitement as she waved her hand and skipped around until the train was out of sight.

"Thaatha, Sai and I will go to the city one day in this train with Nana," said Vidya as Amma screwed up her nose.

"I am sure you will, dear," said Thaatha lovingly. "I will come to meet you there."

"How will you come? You are so scared to board a train," asked Vidya innocently.

"Oh! Don't you worry about that! I will just follow the tracks on my cycle and they will lead me to you."

"That's a good idea!" exclaimed Vidya. "I'd love to come with you on your cycle, but I love the train more, so I will go in the train and you follow it."

CHAPTER 9

A Blessing That Wasn't

Monsoon was about to set in and the pace in the whole village was hectic. There was so much to do. The hut roofs were to be re-laid. The fields were weeded and ploughed, all ready for sowing. Everyone prayed to the rain God.

In the evenings, men and women gathered to sing and dance, praising the Lord of clouds to shower so that they could reap a rich harvest.

All eyes were on the sky as *jhulas* were put on trees. Vidya loved to swing on the *jhulas*. Nana had put one up for her in the verandah on the tamarind tree. She loved to play in the rain, but Amma always worried.

"Vidya, don't get drenched, you will catch a cold," she chided.

But Vidya being Vidya never listened. She just loved the pitter patter and the splash. She would dance in the rain, giggling all the while. Amma had to catch hold of her and get her dry. Oh! It was so much fun. She would then serve hot tea and *pakoras*; delicious *pakoras* in the rain with a cup of tea—what else could one want?

"Let's go to the Devi temple this Tuesday," Nana suggested. It was a ritual that had been followed through generations. "It will be Sai's first visit to the temple, so prepare well." Vidya was excited as always.

As it was Sai's first visit to a temple, there were preparations to be made. Coconuts, flowers and sweets were to be offered to the deity, along with a saree, to seek blessings for the young one. This visit was overdue. Now they would seek the Devi's blessings for the harvest as well.

"I am not feeling very well, why don't you all go and pay your respects to the Devi?" Thaatha said.

"Oh come along, it is just a day. We will start by day break and be back before dark," Nana insisted.

"Dear, I'd love to come along, but I don't think I should this time. My body aches and I feel weak."

It was unusual for Thaatha to say so. He always loved to visit the temples and took Vidya along with him whenever and wherever he went. Nana moved forward and touched Thaatha's forehead gently.

"You're burning up!" he said covering Thaathas's body with the sheet. "We'll go next Tuesday."

"No, don't do that. It's not good to put off the visit to the temple once you've made up your mind. The Devi would not be happy. Go on and pray for me as well. Besides, once the rains start, you will not be able to go. The journey would be difficult, especially with the two young ones."

Nana took a deep breath. "Alright, so we'll start tomorrow, but you must take care," he said, concern obvious in his voice.

"Of course I will. Now don't treat me as if I'm a child who doesn't know any better!" Thaatha never failed to make Vidya smile, not even when he felt ill. He was cheerful as ever. His frail body was curled up but the sparkle in his eyes still hid the pain he must've been in.

Nana went to buy the essentials for the puja on Monday as Amma was busy making sweets. They went to bed early that evening and were up earlier than usual. It was cold, but the sky seemed clear. Amma quickly made some food and packed it in a basket. She left some in the pots for Thaatha.

"Please have something," she urged.

"Of course dear, don't you worry about me. Just go and pray. Pray for health and happiness, for wealth and harvest," he said with a smile as Amma offered him a cup of hot tea with cardamom.

Nana was busy setting up the cart and hitching Bheema to it.

"Aren't Sita and Gauri coming with us?" asked Vidya.

"No dear, let them rest here. We will be back by evening. Bheema is sturdy and he will take us to the temple safely," Nana replied.

"Vidya, come have your bath and milk, we don't have much time," called out Amma as Vidya rushed to her. Sai was all wrapped up cosily and fast asleep.

They set off with the first ray of sun. It looked as if it would be a fine day. There were a few clouds, and the early birds chirped noisily. Soon enough, they passed the lake with the ducks and the ducklings happily swimming around. With fresh air in their lungs, they were all buoyed up and happy.

Vidya felt very pretty in a bright yellow *ghagra* with a maroon blouse. She had worn her favourite bangles which tinkled as she clapped her hands. It was a perfect outing. They would stop under a lush tree in a few hours for tea and breakfast which Amma had packed.

Vidya was already hungry. Amma had made sure she had her milk before they started, but when you are travelling and the journey is good, you always want to munch, hungry or not, and Vidya was just like any child who liked picnics and outings. It did not make any difference if they were making a holy trip to the mandir to offer puja or to her Grandma's place in the neighbouring village. It was all so much fun.

By the time they reached the foot of the hill, the sky was covered in thick dark clouds. The weather had changed drastically. This was not unusual during the monsoons and it was not something to worry about. The Devi Temple was at the top of the hill. They had to make their way up barefoot, leaving the cart at the foot along with the others already there. A few other groups of people from different villages had come that day to pay their respects and seek blessings from the Devi, too. Amma wrapped Sai in an extra layer and gave Vidya an old shawl. She didn't really want it; she wanted to sprint ahead right to the top.

"Vidya, watch your step," Nana called out as he hurried to keep up with her. Amma followed, holding Sai tightly to her bosom.

It would take a few hours to get to the temple. Amma and Nana started to look worried about half-an hour or so into the journey. It had started drizzling and they all wanted to reach the temple before it started to pour. Women covered their heads with their pallus and men with their turban cloth as they started walking briskly. Vidya befriended a few kids and merrily jumped and skipped along, enjoying every moment and the drizzle. The elders sang songs about the glory of the Devi loudly to encourage each other and distract them from the worrisome downpour. They carried fruits, flowers and other offerings in the baskets balanced on their heads.

By the time they reached the temple door, it was pouring. They were all drenched. They still had to wash their feet before they entered the temple. They all gathered around the big well just outside the temple premise. A few young men drew water as the ladies and children were the first to wash and rush under the temple roof with folded hands and shivering bodies.

They then gathered before the deity and as the pundit chanted mantras. Thunder got louder and louder, as if monstrous clouds were crashing together. Vidya moved closer to Nana, clutching his dhoti. Nana pulled her closer to provide her the warmth of his body and much needed security as he sensed her fright. It looked as though the skies had opened their gates and the rumbling giants clashed against each other. It was just past noon, but it was already dark outside. Apart from a few flickering diyas and the lightning that flashed every now and then, one would have thought it was late evening.

The pundit raised his voice, chanting the mantras as though competing with the sound rain and thunder, ringing the golden bell with one hand hastily and performing the aarti at the same time. People huddled together for some respite from the cold. As soon as the puja was done, people put forth their offerings one by one and collected the prasad. Vidya too had her share of prasad. Nana picked her up and moved towards the one corner where it seemed like they might be safe from the splashing water. Amma joined them and they sat down together hugging each other. Sai had been crying for a while, cold and hungry. Amma turned towards the wall and covered Sai with her pallu. Sai suckled hungrily as another deafening strike of thunder filled the air.

"Looks like it's going to really pour today," said a man, coming towards Nana. Even if they were strangers, people were trying to make small talk. They had nothing much to do and were all stuck together in the torrential rain.

"Yes, looks like it. Let's hope it stops soon or we will be stuck here for the night." Nana was worried and it was quite evident.

"Don't worry. You are under Devi's protection. She will take care of all of you," said the priest joining them.

"Gopala, light the fire so that these devotees get some warmth," the priest called to his assistant.

"Right away," answered a young man rushing to a corner and emerging soon with an *angithi* with red hot charcoal.

People gathered around the angithi trying to warm their shivering bodies. Two young pundits came with more angithis as devotees tried to dry their wet clothes.

Amma had brought along some jawar rotis which she shared with Vidya and a few other young kids who ate hungrily. The men wanted to have a puff of beedi to warm up, but as they were taking shelter at the Devi's temple, they had to satisfy themselves with the angithi's heat.

As noon turned into evening, it was clear that the devotees would have to stay at the temple for the night. Punditji had asked the temple servants to prepare some simple food for them. There was worry written all over Nana's face, more so than anybody else's.

"I hope he will be fine," Vidya heard Nana tell Amma in a hushed, worried tone.

"I've been praying all this while. We should have stayed back." She sounded equally worried.

"Did you make enough food for the night?"

"Yes, I did. I hope he has it."

It was obvious that they were worried about Thaatha.

There was more aarti and puja that evening before some hot rice and plain dal was served, which was devoured by all in no time. The night was darker than darkness, only to be lit up by flashes of lightning.

Mothers of young children pulled them close and tried to lull them to sleep, but the temple floor was cold as ice. The sheets offered no relief as the cold wind chilled them to their bones. There were not enough rooms in the Devi temple with its open courtyard with big banyan trees.

"It has not rained like this for 50 years," Vidya heard an old man tell the men in the huddle.

"Devi, have mercy," said another.

There was silence as the downpour gained even more strength; worried faces soon turned into fearful ones. Vidya could not sleep well although Nana made sure that she was on his lap all the while. She woke up with every flash and thunder.

Amma was also worried as Sai's body seemed to get warmer. She had not set him down and had wiped him dry. She sat near the angithi all the time and fed him at frequent intervals. He wasn't crying overmuch, but he seemed much too hot; it was plain that Amma was getting more and more worried as the night went on.

There were silent prayers on every lip and fear in every waking eye. Each person present would talk of this night for a long time to come.

Vidya was scared too, but she felt secure with Amma and Nana beside her. She was also worried about Sai— her little brother Sai. He was so quiet. Amma had let her touch his forehead and it was so hot. How could one be so hot in this cold and rain, she wondered? And instead of being happy that Sai was warm, everyone was so worried. She knew he was unwell as he had not laughed as he always did, did not smile on seeing her face. He was stuck to Amma's chest all the time.

Vidya was young, very young, but she could sense the unending worry of that cold night. The worry brought by the whistling winds, the splashing rain and the thunderstorm, worry about the unusually quiet Sai and Thaatha. She loved him so much and he was all alone in the small hut with Sita and Gauri; but what could the cows do? She hoped he would milk them have a glass of hot milk. Amma always made sure she had milk with turmeric at such times. She drew close to her father as another flash of lightning lit the darkness followed by a crash of thunder.

"Nana," she said in a voice choked with tears.

"Yes, darling."

"Nana . . . Bheema . . ." her voice gave away. "He is out there at the foothill . . . alone in the dark . . . rain . . ."

"Hush!" Nana's voice too choked for the first time.

She had never seen Nana like this before. He quickly regained his composure. "He is sturdy. He is our Bheema. Don't worry. You try and go to sleep."

The night seemed very long as none of them could sleep. It was almost 6 am—they were used to their days starting much earlier. It was still dark outside. The clouds had grown darker and thicker. There was no stopping the rains or the raging wind that threatened to pick them up and toss them aside if they dared to step out of shelter. A few men gathered courage to go and look outside the temple, but to no avail. They could not see anything outside.

Usually, the view from the temple, right at the top of the hill, was mesmerising. One could see the whole village from there; its thick forest, the lush green fields, the lakes and the ponds with its small huts and the *gallis*. It was so picturesque and peaceful. A cool breeze would blow gently, taking away the tiredness of the steep climb and the 700 steps which brought them to the Devi's abode.

"These 700 steps represent seven lives," Nana had told Vidya once, "100 each for each birth."

According to Hindu belief, there are seven births and what you are in your next birth is determined by your Karma.

"When you climb these steps with devotion, the Devi will purify you of all your sins and you can pray to her about your next birth what you want to be; your desires. The Devi always fulfills the wishes of her true devotees."

"But next birth means that you have to die first." Vidya looked worried and sad. There was horror in her innocent eyes.

She slowly got up and walked towards the sanctum sanctorum. The doors were not yet open; the young pundits were already making preparations for the morning aarti. She closed her eyes in front of the door and joined her hands. "Devi," she said in a low voice. "I am Vidya." Her voice quivered. "I was here last year, too. I hope you remember me. I was too little at that time." She paused for a while before continuing. "Devi I am in your temple and Nana says that you take good care of all your true devotees. Devi, I don't want to die. Nana says that you fulfill all the wishes one makes for the next birth, but I want to live this one as well . . . I don't want to die. Please . . . please save me . . . please save me," she whispered, her voice choking with her effort trying to hold back tears which threatened to leak through the dams of the closed lids. "I want to ask you for your blessings in this life itself. I want a good life. I want to become big like Nana wishes me to. I want to have a good life . . . in the city . . . big city . . . . with a big house . . . lots of clothes . . . big car . . . good food."

She seemed to be uttering the words Nana had always spoken. His dream for her.

"Please Devi, bless us all . . . Let me fulfill my father's dream," she said as the sanctum door opened with the ringing of bells. She opened her eyes slowly to take in the majestic sight of Devi in all her grandeur, with her golden crown and smile that seemed to convey something to Vidya. There was love in her eyes. The pundit started chanting mantras loudly, performing the morning aarti as the crowd gathered and the bells rang.

No one had predicted such an onslaught of rain. No one was prepared for it. They had all come to pray for rains and harvest. But this was not what they wanted. It would ruin the harvest. But harvest was not the first cause of worry on their minds. Safety was. Safety for themselves and the loved ones they had left behind in their villages. They knew that the river would have swelled after the night's onslaught. How much, that was their worry. They did not want to speak about it, but everybody wanted the clouds to draw back and the sun's rays to break through so that they could assess the damage. They feared the worst, and hoped they were wrong.

A couple had brought their radio along, but all they could get all night was static. Just the *jjjjjjjsssssssssssshhhhssshhhhhhs* that meant that turning the knob would make no difference. Everyone wanted to listen to the news, wanted to know what had happened. What was going on? But it looked as though there would be nothing but the wind and the rain that would wash everything, including their very existence, away.

Vidya had always loved the rain, but not anymore. She wanted it to stop, stop forever. She wanted to go back home to the comfort of her cosy hut, back with Bheema to Thaatha, Sita and Gauri.

As the day crawled on slowly, punctuated by loud bursts of thunder, there was enough light to offer a glimpse of the world below if you strained the eyes. A few young men walked out of the temple along with Nana hoping to assess how much damage there had been.

After fifteen minutes that seemed like forever, they came back but their faces were grim. The temple was filled with wails of women and men as they described the scene below. The river indeed had swelled to unimaginable proportions and was flowing wild, razing whatever was in its path. The whole village seemed to be underwater. They could barely see any huts below. Trees had been uprooted, they could see none of the familiar landmarks. There was only water, water and more water.

Nana sat down on the floor holding his head. They could not see clearly rain still pouring hard, but they'd seen more than enough. They'd seen the sheer devastation. Devastation like never before, and they were stuck in the Devi's temple with very little or no food. There were women and young children, cold and hungry. At least they were safe, at least for now. But the fate of their loved ones there, down in the villages was uncertain.

The fear of losing everything and everyone is worse than facing your own death. The knock of death is louder than the burst of clouds and its silence was deafening. It is something one never wishes to hear; and today, there wouldn't have been just one knock, they knew it. There would have been knocks; How many? Where all? There gloom was pervasive.

Vidya did not understand the magnitude of what was wrong, but she realised all was not well; not well at all. And they were so helpless, they could do nothing but sit up there on the hilltop, in the Devi's temple watching the destruction below—watch their loved ones suffer from above."I'll go down," Nana said after a long silence. "I have to."

"What?" several people asked.

"My father, he is down there. He is old and sick. I have to go down there," he repeated, getting up.

"And do what?"

It was a commanding voice and people turned instinctively.

"Stop. Stop where you are," continued the pundit, stilling Nana's feet.

"Who do you think you are?" he said in a loud voice. There was silence.

"Do you have the strength to challenge the Gods? To challenge nature?"

"But . . ."

"No buts. It is Devi's *krupa* that we are all safe here in her care. Do you want to disrespect her blessings?"

There was silence again. Not a soul moved, not when the pundit spoke. His voice softened. "I understand your pain. But what can we mortals do in these situations? It is time to safeguard what we have with us." He paused for a while. "Look at them, you mean so much to them. Would you want them lose what they have left? Did you think about that? Just once? What they would do without you? This is life. You have to be practical, very practical."

Amma came close and held Nana's hand tight. Nana burst into tears. He cried loudly, almost louder than the thunder itself. Vidya shrank into a corner. Her eyes filled. She was so scared. She would never forget her father's wail, nor the pundit's words. It would haunt her all her life. *"You have to be practical . . . very practical . . . life has to go on . . . you have to make the best of what is offered . . . ."*

It was on the third day that the heavens seemed to have some pity. No, it did not stop raining, but it was no longer punishing in its strength. They still could not go down to their homes as the river had risen and the currents were still strong. They would stand on the hilltop looking down helplessly. They could feel their warm tears in the cold rain. Vidya too had slipped out quietly once and stood there. The scene that met her eyes was like something out of her scariest nightmares. She ran back into the temple and tried to hide under her mother's pallu.

Sai was a bit better and that was a relief. He had started to smile, but still stuck to Amma. Vidya let him be.

The deafening sound of the helicopter's rotor blades cut through the whistling winds, attracting everyone's attention. They all rushed out looking at the sky as packets were thrown down. There was sudden chaos. Every one rushed to pick the small packets, falling down, pushing, trampling. It was frenetic. Vidya too managed to snatch a few packets. She brought it into the temple and sat down with Amma and Nana. There was food inside it. Very little food and medicine, but it meant a lot at this time – it meant survival.

More helicopters came the next day. This time, along with food, ropes were dropped. People were being air-lifted.

"It means that the situation down there is even grimmer than it looks from here," Nana muttered to himself, loud enough for Amma and Vidya to hear it.

Amma simply held his hand, saying nothing, yet extending the much needed support. It kept them together, the bond strengthened.

When it was Vidya's turn to be airlifted, she screamed. She was scared to death. A strong hand pulled her up. Nana and Amma were also pulled up along with Sai and the chopper flew off to safety.

CHAPTER 10

Ocean Of Grieving Faces

Vidya had always dreamt of the big city; city of dreams. Nana had wished to be there too, but not this way.

It was indeed a beautiful city with clean, wide roads and hundreds of cars, scooters and double-decker buses, with big high-rise buildings and huge supermarkets, where people dressed fashionably. So many ladies had short hair and wore trousers.

They were provided shelter in a relief camp where there were hundreds of people. One tent had to be occupied by many. Most of them had lost all their savings, their homes and their loved ones. It was a sea of grieving faces with sullen eyes and hopeless voices.

Although there were arrangements for food and a few blankets were being distributed along with medicine, there just wasn't enough.

There was confusion and chaos everywhere as politicians and media thronged. Men clad in white clothes and Gandhi *topis* with their big, wobbling bellies seemed to make a mockery and were followed by cameramen as they stopped to speak to the victims. Cameras flashed as brightly as the lightning that had terrified them as the Netas stopped for photo-ops beside scantily clad, crying children.

"I hope you got a good one this time," he said, his voice authoritative.

"Yes, this is a good one," replied a cameraman sounding satisfied with his work.

"Make sure it comes on the front page."

"Sure, Netaji."

And they moved on, stopping wherever there were enough people to make a good audience.

"Netaji, please help us, we are ruined."

"Our homes have been washed away. We have no clothes, no food and no shelter."

"Our children are hungry and sick."

The woes outnumbered the men.

The Neta, clad in his crisp, white kurta, stood listening for some time. He seemed to enjoy the attention. After a while, he cleared his throat and spoke. "I am here for you. I am fully aware of the situation. Your pain is my own," he spoke as loudly as he could to an attentive crowd.

There was something missing in his voice. His words spoke of concern, but there was little conviction or compassion. Yet, people listened to him with rapt attention as the media covered the news.

"I will do whatever I can to ensure more facilities, food, drinking water and medicines."

The speech lasted for a good ten minutes before he folded his hands and walked towards his white Ambassador car with a red light on top.

"Long live Netaji," shouted a supporter who accompanied him.

There were more slogans of "Long live Netaji."

This continued until the car drove away and was out of sight.

Many more Netas came, spoke more or less the same things, posed with crying naked children and old ladies.

Pictures were taken; hopes were built; loud *jaijaikars* echoed and they all drove away in their luxurious fleet of cars

Nana managed to get a bucket of water as Amma washed the kids in half a bucket before going inside a makeshift bath with worn out bed sheets for walls. It had been days and they all smelled like pigs. Most of the flood victims did. The stench was now becoming unbearable. But this was not something to worry about at this time. Their miseries had just started.

It would be days before the water receded and the villages were declared safe to return. People had settled down in the relief camp, but none of the promises made by the big Netas seemed to be fulfilled. As days passed, the flood of journalists and photographers slowed to a trickle, as did the visits of the Netas with crisp white kurta pyjamas and topis.

Food was never sufficient; neither was water nor other basic facilities. Long queues were organised every day, only to be broken when things were distributed. There were fights. It was like a jungle of human animals where the stronger would win and others had to retreat to their tents, dejected.

Vidya had managed to befriend a few children in the camp. She would go out and play with them at times.

"Stay near the tent. Don't wander far," Amma would tell Vidya.

"Amma I am here, don't worry—just here."

"Vidya, this is not our village. It is a city and there are kidnappers here." Amma had been cautioned and she was wary of the surroundings.

Vidya's heart missed a beat. But kids being kids, she would soon forget the warnings as the other children called her to play hopscotch.

CHAPTER 11

Back To The Village

"Y ou stay here with Vidya and Sai. I will come back in a day or two." Nana tried to convince Amma.

"But I cannot stay here all alone in this city," Amma was on the verge to cry. "What if something happens? Who do I have here? How will I take care of both the kids alone?"

"You are not alone here. Sarada and Rohini are with you. Besides, it is much safer here than to come along with me with the kids." Nana's voice was stern. It had to be at this point. "I will come back soon and if everything is fine, we will all go back. You just take care." As Amma seemed to give in, his voice softened. "Punnu, I know you are very courageous. I trust you and I want you to have faith in me."

Punnu was Nana's special pet name for Amma. Her name was Purnima—full moon.

"Alright, but you come soon," she said in a gentle voice, trying to stay strong.

"I am sure father will be fine," she said, hoping to lift his spirits.

"I am sure he will be," he said softly before turning towards Vidya.

"Darling, be a good girl and don't trouble your Amma," he said, ruffling her hair.

"I will be a good girl," Vidya replied. "Come back soon."

"I will, dear," said Nana, handing over a few rupees he had with him to Amma before walking away with a few men from the same village.

Vidya, Amma, Sarada and Rohini stood by the tent watching the men until they were out of sight.

CHAPTER 12

The Mass Cremation

"**A**mma! Amma, where are you?" Vidya called out loudly rushing into the tent as Amma fed Sai.

"What happened, Vidya? What are you shouting for?'

"Amma, Nana is coming!" Vidya cried out excitedly and rushed out before her mother could respond.

All the women rushed out together. The men had promised to come back in two days, but today was the fourth day and they all had been worried. There seemed to be no words to describe their emotions. There was relief that their men had come back, there was hope and uncertainty. What do you call such emotions?

They stood there outside the tent in the relief camp as children ran forward and hugged their fathers. Some men bent down to press a kiss on their forehead, some to lift their children to their shoulders, while some simply held their hands as they walked towards the ladies.

Their faces were grim and their gait was slow and weary. The women shared uneasy glances as their hearts beat louder.

Once inside the tent, the ladies quietly offered water as they all sat down in a huddle. They were eager to know what had happened, but feared what they might hear.

"Children, you go out and play," said one of them.

Vidya went out with the kids, but she did not go to play. She stayed just outside the tent, within earshot, determined to hear what was being said.

"It is all over. All finished. Devi has been furious this year. She has wiped out whatever was in her way." The tale was told with many pauses. "There is no village left. No house, fields, no roads . . ." the voice trailed off as women started to cry. Vidya's heart sank as she thought of Thaatha, Sita, Gauri and Bheema.

Horrendous tales of woe and destruction were unfolded by the men. The extent of devastation had to be seen to be believed. With each story, the wails would grow louder and then turn into sobs as the men continued. Vidya sat down on the floor, arms wrapped tightly around herself. Her cheeks were covered with tears as she sobbed inconsolably.

"Did you find father?"

Vidya's ears pricked as she heard Amma ask the question.

There was an eerie silence before Nana spoke.

"The gales were strong and father weak, very weak with fever." He stopped for a while as though taking control of his emotions. "As the rainstorm showed its strength, men and women scampered into their houses, hoping that the skies would have mercy. But the water rushed into the village, fields and then their homes. They tried to save themselves. Some tried to pack up what they could and reach higher ground some way. The young people and children ran as fast as they could, the women following them. A few were fortunate, but the majority were not—the water rose too high, too fast."

Pausing for a while as the crowd listened, he went on. "Ramanna had come to visit father as he knew that he was alone and sick." There was pain in his voice, but he controlled himself and continued. "They both sat near the sigree as it rained continuously. Father's body was burning up and he shivered even though he was covered with blankets and the fire was ablaze. The winds blew furiously as the trees bent to their will; some of them were uprooted. Our thatched roof had started to leak and darkness had descended."

It was as though he was speaking to himself.

"They both knew well that they could not wade through the heavy currents to reach higher land. It was when the roof was blown away that they decided to climb up the tamarind tree in hope of safety."

His voice choked slightly at this point.

"People who had stayed back hoping for the rains to stop had already started climbing the trees. Ramanna helped father climb the branches, but not before he untied Sita and Gauri, who ran helter-skelter. As the cloudburst and winds grew stronger, they kept hearing the sound of trees falling down, with the people in them. It was pitch dark and the gales so strong that one could barely hear the screams in the open with the skies pouring. Father was feeble. He could not hold on for long. He felt his grip loosen. He took out his dhoti and tied himself tightly to the branch on which he sat. The night seemed endless. As dawn broke, it was a horrifying scene. The huts were submerged as strong currents flowed. There were uprooted trees, roof tops, bloated cattle and bodies all floating around—destruction. It needed courage to see the gory scenes that nature unveiled that morning. Time crawled and seemed to stand still as the day progressed. Weak and hungry, burning in the pouring rain, father and Ramanna held on for dear life. They prayed to God to have mercy as darkness engulfed them again."

There were gasps and cries as Nana continued.

"On the third day, when the water receded a little, Ramanna tried to check on father as he had not spoken for a long time. Old age coupled with sickness, hunger and cold had taken its toll."

Describing what he had heard from Ramanna, Nana continued. "Father's body had to be brought down to be cremated in the mass cremation." He broke down, as did Amma.

Vidya was shaken to her very core as she cried out loudly, but there was so much going on that her cries went unnoticed.

"I could not even get the honour of giving fire to my father's pyre. I could not even disperse his *asthis*." Nana's courage seemed to give away as he cried aloud.

Vidya had seen too much and too soon. Her father was a pillar of strength and she was seeing him break down. She had never imagined he could shatter like this. She felt like running to him and wiping away his tears, but could not move. She felt helpless. She felt a part of her break; a part that never came together again.

"When are we going back home?" Amma asked between sobs.

"Not soon, not in the near future." Nana's voice sounded frail and very tired.

"Why?"

"It's not safe yet. There is sickness all around. We have to give the village time to heal. It will take time . . . it will take time."

"What will we do till then?"

"We will have to look for some work, whatever we get. We have no choice."

That night Vidya did not sleep much, nor did the others. Whenever she dozed off, she was woken by bad dreams, dreams of thunderstorms. Dreams of Thaatha being swept away.

CHAPTER 13

An Unwilling Journey

Reality hit them like boulders. People had no choice but to accept facts and move on as well as they could. They could not stay in the relief camp forever. Conditions were worsening. Men and women now started searching for jobs. They needed money to keep themselves and their children alive. Slowly, people started moving out of the camp.

"Punnu, be ready by six in the morning, we are moving out," Nana told Amma as soon as he came in that evening.

"Where are we going? Have you found some work?"

"Yes, on the outskirts of the city. There are buildings being constructed and I have spoken to the *maistiry* who has agreed to give both of us some work at the construction site."

"Construction site?" Amma was surprised. She was a farmer's wife and daughter. What could she do at a construction site, she wondered aloud

"Work is work, Punnu. We have to be thankful we got a job. You can break the stones and I will have to do whatever is needed."

Amma looked worried.

"Don't worry much, we will learn. We will be able to keep any eye on the children as well while we are at work," he assured. "We can build a small hut on the nearby vacant land. It will all be fine."

Most of the villagers had found odd jobs in the markets, pulling rickshaws or at the station as coolies. They would go early in the morning and come back at dusk. Amma had hoped to stay with the villagers where she felt safe and connected, but Nana explained.

"See Punnu, all these people have a new struggle every day. They may or may not get work. There is no guarantee how much they earn by the evening; and if they don't find a job, they may not have anything to eat for the day. We will be working with the maistiry until the construction is complete, which will take at least three to four years. We will have a steady job and daily wages. I'm sure you will be able to befriend the other women workers. Think positive dear, it will all be fine. Remember what Punditji said. *This is life. You have to be practical . . . very practical.*"

Amma felt better. She knew it would be difficult, but there was hope. As soon as the village is safe, we will go back anyway, she thought.

CHAPTER 14

The Journey Continues

After a few hurried goodbyes, they caught an early bus from outside the camp the next day. It was Vidya's first time ever on a bus. She ran up and sat by a window as came and Amma sat next to her with little Sai on her lap. Nana sat behind as the conductor came towards them.

Nana handed some coins to the conductor, who gave tickets.

"Let me know when the stop comes, I am new to here," Nana requested the conductor, who nodded and moved ahead.

Vidya loved the journey as they passed the high-rise buildings on broad, black, tarred roads. There were newspaper boys and milkmen on cycles. The sweepers were still sweeping as the lazy city slowly rose for the day. The morning market was full of fresh green vegetables. It had been days since Vidya and her family had had a good meal cooked by Amma. Looking at the vegetables, she cried out, "Amma, look at the potatoes and greens, can we buy some? You can make sambhar and rice today; it's been so long you cooked good food."

"Yes dear, once we reach our destination, I will definitely cook tasty food," Amma replied lovingly.

Vidya was happy. She had hated vegetables, but now she missed them. She missed the mango pickle and *rasam*, but Amma had said she would cook again, and Vidya was happy.

It was a long journey. As the day went on, the roads were swarmed with people and traffic; the bus was so crowded. It was sultry and hot. As the bus stopped briefly, more people got in than got out. Vidya was happy to be seated near the window as breeze blew. She was fascinated by the big hoardings with pictures of beautiful women in the finest of silk and jewellery. They looked lovelier than the most beautiful brides she had seen in her village.

The shops were opening for business and she could see toys, big blue buses, red cars, teddy bears and dolls. She had never seen so many toys even in the village mela. She clapped her hands in joy as amused passengers looked at her. She became self-conscious and sat upright. There were stern faces all around. No one greeted each other, there were no smiles. The women dressed like men in shirts and trousers; they had short hair and painted lips. Men seemed to have long hair. They seemed to be in a hurry. No one seemed to enjoy the ride. Vidya was amused. "How strange," she thought as she lost herself again to the view outside.

As the bus went on, the buildings became smaller, the roads narrower and less crowded. The conductor pulled the rope which rang a bell and the driver stopped the bus, letting passengers get down. It now looked more like her village, with green fields. She could see the mynahs and kingfishers perched on the electric wires which seemed to be travel endlessly with her. She could now feel the freshness in the air. The bus was almost empty with only a few seats occupied. Sai had been sleeping all along. She gave him a loving smile, ruffling his hair, and then leaned closer to gently kiss his cheek. He looked so beautiful. Amma smiled back.

"Wake up, honey; we have to get down here." Nana's voice woke Vidya.

She did not remember falling asleep. She woke up with a start and hurried towards the exit as the bus slowed and then came to a halt. They were at a small, dilapidated old bus stop. It was mid afternoon and they were all sweating. As the bus moved on, they were engulfed in smoke and dust. Gone were the tar roads and the high-rise buildings. The place looked deserted, with not a soul in sight. It was barren, with a few bushes and bare trees lining the *kuchcha* road.

Amma looked at Nana quizzically as Vidya came closer to hold her hand.

"Don't worry; we are at the right place. The maistiry has promised to send someone who will take us to the construction site from here. I am sure he will come soon," Nana said, taking Sai from Amma.

They then carried their belongings towards the bus stop and sat on the cement bench. The bench was so hot that Vidya jumped up as soon as she sat down. Amma bent down to pour some water from the mud *surai* she was carrying. Little Sai also had a small drink from the little glass. They sat there silently for a good half hour before they saw an old man in a bullock cart with lazy bulls dragging their feet in the hot sun. All eyes were anxious as he came closer.

"Venkatlu?" asked the old man.

"Yes"

"I am Satya. Come, hop on, *Dora* sent me to pick you up," he said, getting off the cart to help them with their luggage. He reminded Vidya of her grandfather.

Nana quickly picked up the bundles and loaded the cart before Amma got in along with Sai.

Vidya stopped by the bull, patting it with love as her heart filled with pain and her eyes with tears. Bheema was much stronger, more robust.

"What's his name, Satya Thaatha?" she asked gently.

"Shyamu," replied the old man. "Do you like him?"

Vidya did not reply.

"Come darling, let's go, it's hot out here" Nana said gently as he lifted Vidya and placed her in the cart. He had sensed her feelings, but chose not to say much at the moment. He didn't need to, so close were they to each other. They always knew.

Nana sat in the front along with Satya, asking him many questions. Amma listened to them with rapt attention, while Vidya and Sai played with each other.

It took them an hour and a half to reach the construction site. There was dust all around as the hot sun beat down mercilessly. Men and women were all covered in sweat and dust as they carried bricks, sand and cement on their heads in *gampas*. A few children played in the shade of the scattered trees under the workers' watchful eyes.

Vidya and Amma were tired out by the jerky journey. Sai had become cranky and started to cry. He was uncomfortable. Amma lifted him and gave him a sip of water, which he drank greedily.

CHAPTER 15

An Unfinished City

"Come, let me take you to Dora," Thaatha said walking towards the rudimentary structure of a building.

The building was huge. It was nothing like they had ever seen before, not even in the city.

"What construction is going on here? This looks like a huge building."

"A steel factory is going to come up here soon," Satya replied.

"Here? In this barren land where there is no sign of civilisation?" Amma was surprised as was Nana.

"Yes. Here." replied Satya. "In a few years' time, this place is going to be very different. It is going to develop very fast. Thousands of engineers and workers are going to come and settle down here."

Satya continued as he walked towards the building with Nana with Amma following him closely.

"You see those small buildings there?" he pointed in another direction. "Those are going to be the workers' quarters."

It looked like an unfinished city—an evolving town.

"There is going to be lots of greenery. Dora has specially ordered for grass and plants, which will be planted sometime before completion of the factory. Lots of opportunities coming up."

They entered the building, and there was a big wooden table with foldable tin chairs in the room. On one of the chairs sat a huge man. He must have been about Venkatlu's age, but he was big, with a huge belly and a very tanned. He wore a thick gold chain and a stone-studded ring on each finger. Each ring had a different stone. One even had seven stones – a big square ring you couldn't help noticing. Venkatlu kept his belongings down and folded his hands.

"So, how was the journey?" asked the big-bellied man, peeping through his spectacles.

"It was fine."

"Oh Nana, it wasn't," thought Vidya to herself.

"Go along with Satya. Make yourself comfortable today. You need to start work in the morning."

"Yes, Dora."

"Satya, show them around. Help them settle down and explain the work to them."

"Yes, Dora," replied Satya, as Nana picked his belongings up again and followed.

They were led to the other side of the construction site. What a stark contrast to huge building! There were bamboo huts with coconut thatch—hundreds of them with very narrow lanes, so narrow that if you stretched your arms out, you could touch the huts on both sides. In some a few children and women could be seen. Amma nervously smiled at them as they smiled back.

They walked through the winding, confusing lanes. It was like a maze. "Oh God! How will I remember these lanes?" thought Vidya. The huts were all so like each other, as were the lanes with dirty water flowing through them.

After what seemed a very long time, they stopped somewhere in the centre of the hut village.

"Here, this is going to be your new home. Make yourselves comfortable. Rest well. I will meet you tomorrow at six in the morning. Be ready by then." Satya stood outside, as the family entered their new dwelling. There was just one room, big enough to accommodate the family of four. The floor had to be swept and the roof needed repair. There was no door, just an opening in the wall.

Amma looked at Nana.

"How did you like it?" Satya asked.

"It's good. Very good. Thank you very much," replied Nana.

Vidya looked at Nana again. This was the second time in a day that Nana had not been honest. He had never lied before. Vidya was confused, but did not say a word. She was too tired.

"Alright then, you can draw water from the well right at the end of this lane. There is also a small grocery shop down there. You will find all essentials. Come, let me show you the place."

Nana followed Satya as Amma gently handed Sai to Vidya and started cleaning the floor with a small broom she found lying in the hut.

"Amma, it is so dirty here."

"Hush Vidya, I will clean up the place. Just hold Sai carefully."

"Amma, I am hungry."

"Yes darling, let me just clean this place a little bit, and then I will give you rotis."

By the time Amma cleaned the hut and placed their belongings in a corner, Nana returned with two pots and a little rice and vegetables. Amma placed the only mat they had on the floor as Vidya sat down.

"I'll go fetch some water," Nana said. 'Let's clean up a little and rest before we start work tomorrow."

"This roof needs repair. The sun is shining through it."
Nana looked up at the roof.

"Hmmm. Let me see what can be done." He picked
up the pots he had brought and walked out of the hut.

After a wash and a quick meal, Vidya dozed off.
When she woke up, it was evening. The roof had been
fixed with fresh coconut leaves and Amma's saree
covered the hut's 'door'. Vidya stepped out and found
lots of kids running around, shouting and waving in the
lane outside. They stopped when they saw Vidya. Vidya
smiled at them, they smiled back at her. People were now
returning from work, the sun was setting, and the heat
was a little less punishing, but they still sweated.

CHAPTER 16

Every Penny Counts

When Vidya woke up the next morning, she missed the chugging train, the tinkling bells, the cool breeze and the open fields.

Amma and Nana were up. Amma had also finished cooking for the day. She was packing lunch for herself and Nana.

"Where do we leave the kids? We cannot take them out in the open scorching sun."

"Relax, there must be some way. Let Satya Thaatha come, I will find out. There are hundreds of families with children. There must be some arrangement."

Satya Thaatha came at six sharp as promised.

"So, all ready? I see you've settled in well," he said glancing around the hut.

"Yes. Thank you. However, we have a small problem."

"And what's that?"

"My children are too young to be left alone in this new place, and it gets too hot in the afternoons to bring them along."

"Oh, that. Don't worry. We have an arrangement for the workers and families here. There is a small school; well, not exactly a school, but there is something like that, where people leave their children in the morning and pick them up on their way back home."

Amma and Nana looked at each other and then at Vidya.

"Come, let me show you the place before we leave for work. Come on, hurry up, you wouldn't like to be late on the first day itself."

"But . . ."

Thaatha did not let Amma finish her sentence.

"Don't worry. It will all be fine. There are a few old ladies there who take care of the children. Come and check it out yourself. Besides, you've come here to work, and some adjustments need to be made."

"Come on, hurry up."

Vidya was unhappy. She loved going to school. But that was her school in the village where she had friends. She had books she loved.

As though reading her thoughts, Nana came and held her hand. "Come, dear, it's going to be fine. I'm sure you will love the place. You will make friends."

The school was in an open place. It was not like an actual school, but three big huts where small boys in **banians** and **chaddis** and girls in skirts and tops sat on the floor. A few of them wailing, some of them playing with each other, while some of them just sat there with empty eyes.

On seeing them, a lady who seemed to be in her mid-fifties approached. "So, this is the new family you brought in yesterday?"

"Yes. They are very good, and this is their daughter . . ."

"Vidya. She is Vidya and this is Sai," Nana completed the sentence.

"Oh, she's so lovely. Come Vidya, I'm sure you will enjoy being here. See, there are so many children"

"But Sai?" Amma was visibly anxious as she tried to see into the hut and what it was like.

"Don't worry, he will be well taken care of."

"This is Swarna. She and a few other elderly ladies take care of the children," Satya Thaatha tried to assure Amma.

Swarna stepped forward to hold Amma's hand, assuring her. Amma's eyes were moist and Vidya looked very nervous.

"I will be with them throughout the day. I will make sure your kids are comfortable. Don't worry, you go to work." She took Sai from Amma's arms. Vidya leaped and took Sai in hers, almost snatching him.

"Okay, okay. Sai will be with you. I will just be around." Swarna smiled.

Vidya looked nervously at her parents, holding tightly on to Sai.

"Vidya, be a good girl, take care of Sai." Amma hugged Vidya.

"Of course she will. She always does," Nana said, but he sounded equally worried.

Very soon, it became routine. Amma and Nana would leave the kids at the school on their way to work and pick them up on their way back. Vidya too made friends. However, it was more of a day care than a school. The caretaker ladies would tell stories, make sure they had their lunch, and put them to sleep in the noon so that they did not run around in the scorching sun before their parents came to take them home.

Days turned into weeks, then into months. It had been almost seven months since they came there. The family tried to save as much as they could in the hope that they could go back to their village, to their farm, where they would again sow seeds and pray for a good harvest. But it would take a lot more time now. They did not have Sita, Gauri and Bheema. They had to save every penny. They toiled every day.

As the days passed, Venkatlu earned the respect of the workers and trust of the maistiry. Amma would sieve the sand and carry bricks on her head in a gampa, but Nana learnt the skills well. He was hard-working. He learnt the work of bricklaying, which fetched him a little more money.

Although Amma too made friends with the other ladies, but they were not like her village friends in whom she trusted blindly and with whom she shared all small things. She always found something amiss.

CHAPTER 17

The Fall

It had been about two hours since Vidya and Sai got to school. It was the beginning of yet another sunny day. She listened to one of the stories the caretaker told. The day had hardly begun.

"Vidya, come child, you need to go home." It was Swarna.

"But we just came."

"No questions. Just follow me and take Sai along."

"But she's in the middle of the story."

"Vidya, just come. Quick," Swarna's voice was stern and urgent, flat. She was not angry, but there was something wrong that Vidya did not quite understand. She quietly lifted Sai up and walked behind Swarna.

"What happened?" the caretaker asked.

"You continue your story. Take care of the kids," Swarna replied before holding Vidya's little hand and walking briskly out of the room.

They did not speak, but Vidya realised they were going back home.

"Why are we going home? Amma and Nana won't be at home yet."

"You need to go to the city."

"City? Why?"

"Look dear, just follow me, and walk faster, there's no time to talk. And yes, you are a good girl. Very strong, very brave."

"Why are you saying all this? How have I been brave?"

"Darling, you need to take care of your brother and Amma. Give her strength."

"Give Amma strength? Why? What happened to her?"

"Nothing, just follow me."

Vidya was confused, and getting scared. Something was wrong. Fear quickened her steps. Vidya was almost running. She could hear her heart pound.

As they entered the gully, Vidya could see a large group of people gathered near their hut. She shook her hand free and ran towards the crowd.

"Amma, Amma," she was crying. She was frightened, a nameless sense of foreboding rising in her heart.

There was a dump truck waiting at the corner. As she tried to enter the hut, Satya Thaatha held her hand. "Here, darling, this way." He led her towards the truck.

There was so much confusion. As she made way through the throng she could feel them looking at her strangely. Some tried to smile and patted her head, as though trying to say something, trying to console her, give her strength.

Amma was sitting in the truck as Thaatha took Sai from Vidya's arms and handed him over to Amma. Amma was crying too. But why? Before she could ask any question, Vidya was lifted and put in the trolley.

"Come on quick, quick, start moving."

There was a jerk as the vehicle started and Vidya almost fell down. It was then that she saw her father, her Nana, lying there, covered in blood. There were a few more workers in the truck. Nana did not move. His eyes were closed and there was too much blood.

"Nana, Nana!" shrieked Vidya. "Amma! What happened to Nana?"

Amma was crying. She pulled Vidya close to her bosom and held her tight. She did not say anything. It seemed as if she couldn't say anything. Sai started crying too.

It was a very long journey. "Have a sip of water, sister." "Have courage." "It will all be fine." "Don't worry." People tried to comfort them, but they didn't even notice who said what. All that mattered was that they should go as fast as they could.

The city was so far away that even if they went as fast as they could, it would take ages, much too long. Vidya sat there holding on to Amma's hand, but her eyes never left her father's face.

"Nana, Nana, please say something, please. It's me, your Vidya. Please . . . ." she whispered as though speaking to herself. "God, please, please . . . I will never ask for new clothes for Diwali. I won't even ask for sweets. I promise. I will pray every day. I will be a good girl. Please make Nana speak to me, please!" she whispered entreaties and promises, willing to give anything if only Nana would speak to her.

After an eternity, the trolley stopped and the men jumped out. They lifted Nana and rushed him inside the city hospital. Amma followed them quickly, carrying Sai, as Vidya ran along, trying to keep up. There were nurses in white coats and caps, and the doctors in white coats with stethoscopes around their neck.

'Doctor, doctor, please take a look here, our co-worker is hurt. He needs attention fast."

Before the doctor could take a step forward, Amma fell at his feet.

"Please, please save my husband. He is the only one we have. We love him, we need him. Please save him," she pleaded.

Vidya might have been too young to understand what was happening, but she realised that this man could save her father's life. She too fell at his feet. "Please, doctor. Doctor, my Nana."

"Please let go of my feet. Let me have a look. If you hold me like this, how will I treat the patient?"

Vidya did not want to let go of those feet. She felt as though she was holding god's feet. She was holding on to hope. She was holding on to Nana's life. The doctor freed himself and went towards the lifeless Nana.

"What happened?" he asked, keeping his face blank.

"He was working at the construction site, laying bricks, when he slipped and fell down." There was a pause. "From the fifth floor," said a voice.

"It's a police case then. Have you filed a report?"

"Doctor, we are coming straight to you to save our friend."

"Ok, then we will have to inform them. I cannot touch this case until the formalities are taken care of.'

"Doctor, it might be too late by then."

The doctor went to the telephone at the reception and spoke to someone for about two minutes.

"Sister, quick. Take him to the operation theatre. Quick!"

Everyone moved like lightning, taking Nana with them.

"Nana . . . Nana . . ."

Vidya wanted to go with Nana, as did Amma, but a few hands held them back. Faces blurred as people tried to console them, but they stood there like statues, staring at the door that had swung shut after Nana was rushed inside.

"Fifth floor? What does fifth floor mean? How can Nana fall off the fifth floor?" Vidya had heard of falling off a tree, falling off the cycle, falling down when running; but what was falling off the fifth floor?

It couldn't have been more than ten minutes before the doctor came out of the operation theatre. His face was grim. He walked towards them as the men who had come along stood up and looked at him anxiously.

Every word he spoke took time to reach their ears. "I'm sorry." The doctor paused. "It was an hour too late. I could not save him."

"What do you mean, an hour late? He was not going to school to be late. What do you mean by late?" Vidya was not sure if she spoke those words aloud or in her mind.

Amma shrieked and fell down, fainting. Sai started wailing. Vidya stood there, looking around, lost and confused. She did not move. She stood there for a while, then slowly turned towards the operation theatre and ran as fast as she could to her Nana. "Nana! Nana, wake up See what happened to Amma, she has fallen down. Nana, wake up . . . Nana . . . Nana . . . Nana . . ." Her futile cries turned into whimpers.

All she remembered after that was people talking about money needed for cremation. Amma didn't have much. The other workers were also poor and had accompanied the family in a hurry. They hadn't brought much.

The police arrived by then and started taking statements. Amma was in no position to talk. The case was recorded as 'Dead On Arrival'.

"I think we will need to call the Municipality," said a person after a long pause. "There is not much we can do about this."

"Yes, that looks like the best option," said another.

"Who is Municipality?" Vidya asked Amma, who was still in shock.

"Sister, we want to do a lot, but you understand the situation. It would not be wise to carry the body all the way back, and even if we go back, the problem would be the same."

"We have collected a few rupees, it will be enough. At least the Municipality will ensure that the rites are done properly."

"Body? What body? Who Municipality?"

Vidya got no answers to her questions. In fact, no one was listening to her.

"Sister, please say something. The hospital will not keep the body here forever. We need to act fast. If you agree, the cremation will be done by sunset."

Amma sat on the floor, eyes vacant, oblivious. One of the nurses shook her shoulder; she shrieked and fainted again.

"We need to take matters in our hands now," said one of the elderly men in a low but matter-of-fact voice. "She is in no state to make decisions. We must do what is best at this hour. Go call the Municipality."

A few women had also gathered by then. Vidya got to know about the accident through their hush-hush conversations. All of them were inquisitive.

"What happened?"

"Oh, the poor woman! She is so young."

"Two kids to look after."

"What will she do now?"

So many questions. So much discussion. Vidya stood there like a spectator, watching as her worst nightmare unfolded before her. She did not know how she felt, but it hurt. It hurt deep and it hurt a lot.

A few men came in a van. "Where is the body?"

'There," pointed one of the men.

It was then Vidya realised what they meant by body.

"It is my Nana. He is not a body," she was shouting. Her voice quivered with anger as tears flowed down her cheeks. She did not wipe them away. She ran towards the men who were lifting Nana. She wanted to stop them, but she couldn't, she was too small. She ran towards Amma.

"Amma stop them. Please stop them. They are taking Nana. Amma, why don't you say something! Amma, Amma!"

Vidya was furious. She started hitting Amma with her small palms, making contact with her face, bringing her back to bleak reality.

"Amma, Nana!" Vidya sobbed.

"Stop. Stop! Don't take him. Stop!" Amma sprang up, and Vidya followed.

CHAPTER 18

To Bones and Ashes

They were taken to a *shamshaan* where a few old ladies forcefully broke Amma's bangles. Amma was wailing. A few ladies held her while another wiped her bindi and *sindoor*. The broken bangles had pierced Amma's wrists in the struggle and they was bleeding.

"Why are you hurting Amma? Why are you breaking her bangles?"

"It is all fate."

"Pray for the departed soul."

"You need to be strong for the sake of your kids."

"Cry, woman, cry your heart out!"

So many people. So many words. Bitter words. Words that hurt instead of providing solace.

It was too much for Vidya to handle.

Vidya's father was then laid on the pyre and little Sai was made to light it.

There were more cries. Amma fainted again.

"You are burning my Nana. You bad people. Nana, Nana, get up, wake up! These people are burning you. Get up, please!"

Vidya was held tightly as she struggled. She fought. She used all her strength. She tried biting the hands that held her, but then did not loosen. Her wrists hurt. She could not free herself and slowly, all that remained of

Nana was ash. Nana was gone. All that remained was the smell of burnt flesh and ashes.

Amma fainted again. Who could've thought that such would be the end of the sunny day? Nana had left Vidya and Sai at the school that morning. She had hugged Nana and asked him to bring her new clothes and sweets for Diwali, just a few days away. The festival of light; the festival where she would burst crackers and burn *phuljharis*, and here, she had to see people burn her Nana and she could do nothing about it. Nothing at all.

Vidya did not remember what happened next. She was too tired, too drained – there had been more fear, sadness, helplessness than her little body could contain that day. She woke up the next morning with swollen eyes and emptiness in her heart, an emptiness that would never leave her. Amma looked equally helpless as she sat beside her, feeding Sai a glass of milk someone had offered. She had not slept. Vidya could see the same emptiness in Amma's eyes as well. She slowly moved towards Amma and sat down beside her quietly.

CHAPTER 19

The Dampened Lights

Most of the people soon went back.

"We need to get back to work. Our wages will be docked if we don't."

They had their families to look after. Amma had to stay behind to collect Nana's asthis and perform the last few rituals. Hari, one of the workers at the construction site, decided to stay back to help Amma.

"I want to go back to my village." Amma spoke after a long silence.

"Alright, I will try and make some arrangements."

"Hari, could you arrange for me to go to the neighbouring village instead?"

"Sure. But why there?"

"That's where my brothers live . . . lived." Amma's voice faltered.

"What do you mean by that?"

"I don't know if they have come back. Those floods affected all the villages. I have had no news of them since then."

"Then what will you do there?"

"I hope I find them there. They will help me and my children."

"Did you not try to find out what'd happened to them earlier?"

"There was no way. We were all caught in the same situation. All that I know is that my elder brother escaped the floods with his family and was in another town. I am hoping they are back in the village by now."

"What if you don't find them there?"

Amma was silent once again.

"Ok, don't worry. Let us first finish the rituals, go back to the factory and get your belongings, then we can plan how you can go back to your village."

"Yes. I will have to go back to the factory. There is not much to collect, but yes, a few clothes and his belongings. His photo . . . our one and only family photo." Amma's eyes filled again. She no longer wailed or screamed, but the pain was still there, in all its fierce intensity.

"Hari, I have only Rs. 50 left with me. Do you think it will be enough?"

"Enough for the puja and the ticket back to the factory." He paused, thinking for a few minutes and said, "You may have to stay back for a few days. Go back to work, save something before your journey back home."

"Save? Save for going back home? That's exactly what we were trying to do, and see what happened?" There was anger in her voice as she sobbed. "If only if we had gone back. If only! He'd still be with us."

"Take heart. You can't change or undo what's done."

But all words seemed empty. There was no solace – it was a pain that ate away at her very soul. It felt as if it would never ease.

They stayed close to the temple for the next few days. The devotees offered food, blankets and sweets. Diwali was approaching. Light, celebration and happiness were all around, but the festive spirit didn't touch Purnima or Vidya.

CHAPTER 20

Unending Agony

The journey back to the factory was the most difficult. Vidya remembered the last time she had travelled there. Nana had been with them. She had loved the high-rise buildings, the broad roads, had been fascinated by the big shops with all goodies. They were in a similar bus, on the same road. She'd never thought that the same journey could be so different. Everyone was quiet as the bus rumbled along the dusty road.

It was almost evening when they reached the factory. People were winding up work. A few of them came forward on seeing them.

"How are you now Punnu?" asked an elderly woman.

"You need to be courageous for the sake of your children," said another.

Amma silently kept nodding her head. It was like an endless loop; the same dialogues over and over again. It frustrated Vidya.

"Make way for Dora," said someone from the crowd as the maistiry came forward.

"So, you've come back again?" he asked rudely.

Amma nodded.

"Good. Take your belongings and move out as fast as you can."

There were hushed whispers and disbelief on faces as Amma looked at him, confused. She had just lost her husband; she was in grief and helpless.

"But Dora," she pleaded.

"Not a single word. I know what you are going to say." He paused for a while. "Don't even think of coming to me for compensation. That husband of yours, he was kept here as a labourer, but he could never be content. Wanted to do big things. Who asked him to go up there and fall?" His voice was loud. Vidya moved to grab hold of Amma's hand.

"But Dora, you only allowed him to . . ." started one of the labours, but was cut short.

"Allowed him to do what? Fall down and put me in such a situation? I have had enough of the police in the past few days, and I am making one thing clear. I don't want any further nuisance or trouble." He paused for a second, looking at the crowd that had gathered. "And people who want to go against me can pack their bags as well."

He left as quickly as he'd come, leaving the helpless family behind him. The crowd dispersed quietly.

Amma had no choice but to leave, but she had to wait until the next morning as there was no bus until then.

"I'm going to the city tomorrow to bring some material. I will leave you there," offered Satya.

"But I don't have money for the tickets."

"I am going in the lorry. You can come along. We need to leave early, so be ready." There was not much Satya Thaatha could, either. He too was an insignificant labourer earning his living at the construction site. Amma was thankful to him.

When money speaks, it commands, and with Venkatlu's family out of way, there was nobody to claim any damages or compensation. The case was easily buried as suicide.

CHAPTER 21

Struggle For Life

Being back in the city, knowing no one, having no money, with two small children in tow, just after losing her husband—it was a difficult situation. Amma did not have support. No one to console her. No one to turn to for guidance.

"God, why him? You could have taken my life. What shall I do now? Where shall we go?"

Vidya was no longer the bright, chirpy girl she used to be. She had become very quiet. She had no answers, and was scared. She tried to help Amma by taking care of Sai and following her wherever she went.

For the time being, Amma went back to the temple. She sat there along with her kids as the devotees offered food. They were poor but they had always worked hard. They were not beggars, but had no choice at the moment.

"You new here?" asked a woman sitting beside Amma.

"Yes."

"Ok, so, you've come for Darshan?"

"No."

"Then?"

"I need some shelter for some time."

The old lady must have been in her 60s. Her clothes were unwashed and she smelled unclean. Her uncombed hair, covered by her pallu, was all tangled up. She had a big dirty bandage with blood stains wrapped on her left foot which she had stretched out for public view.

"Are you alone here? Where is your husband?"

Amma's eyes filled again. Slowly, as the evening turned darker Amma wept and told her everything. The old lady's voice turned soft as she consoled Amma, wiping her tears.

"You will need Gangu's permission to stay here," she said.

"Gangu?"

"Yes, he is the one who permits people to stay here. If it was for a day or two, you could have stayed in the temple premises, but you will need some work as well to feed your children and to save money to go back home."

"Why do I need Gangu's permission to stay here?"

"We all need it. We give him *hafta* and he permits us to beg here and earn a living."

"I don't want to beg. We are not beggars."

"In that case, he will find you some work."

Amma did not know what to do, what to say. That night they slept on the temple steps. It must have been past midnight when the old lady came and woke Amma. Vidya too woke up.

"Come with me. Let me take you to Gangu."

"Now?" Amma was surprised and scared.

"Yes. Now. He comes only at this hour. This is the right time for you to meet him."

"My children?"

"Let them stay here. You meet Gangu, tell him all about yourself. I am sure he will get you some work."

"Vidya, take care of Sai. I'll come back soon."

Vidya sat beside Sai. She did not want to be left alone in the dark, out in the open. As Amma walked hesitantly with the old lady, Vidya turned towards the shrine, folded her trembling hands and said a silent prayer.

The young widow had been given no time to grieve.

Sai had fallen sick. He had not had milk since the evening before. His body was much too hot and Amma was worried.

"Come lady, time to go to work."

"But my son is not well. How can I leave him and come? It's going to be dark soon. Do I have to work at this hour?"

"Yes. And besides, only if you work will you be able to get him some medicine. You go to the same place. Gangu is waiting for you there and I will stay here with the children."

Amma did not want to leave.

"Go now. I am here with them."

Vidya was scared again. She did not want to be left alone with Sai. The old lady was with them, but Vidya did not like her.

Amma came back after a few hours. There was a bottle of tonic in her hand.

"Vidya, hold Sai, let me put some of this in his mouth."

"Where did you go Amma?"

"Amma's got work selling balloons."

"Okay."

"Vidya, we will soon go back home. You don't worry. You just need to take care of Sai when I am at work."

"But, he is not well. He cries all the time. I am unable to take care."

"This medicine should work."

Until Diwali, Amma sold balloons, but the money she got was not sufficient for food and medicine for Sai, who seemed to be getting worse. She only got some commission by selling them. Most of her earnings went to Gangu. After all, it was his investment and she had to pay him back. With Diwali gone, there weren't too many people—no small kids to sell balloons to. Amma was worried again.

"These balloons don't sell anymore. Will you ask Gangu to get me some other work?" she asked the old lady.

"Let me see. I will talk to him."

"I am ready to do anything."

"Okay," said the old lady looking at Amma from head to toe.

That evening, Sai would not stop crying. The tonic Amma had brought was over. It hadn't done much good. He did not want to leave Amma's side.

"Amma, please stay. Please don't go today," Vidya urged.

"I will come back soon darling. I need to go to work. I will bring more tonic. We will take Sai to the doctor tomorrow." Saying this, Amma walked away hurriedly. Vidya was left there to take care of the little one.

CHAPTER 22

The Final Blow

Amma did not come back that night. Sai's condition had worsened. They had no real shelter and it had started drizzling. Vidya picked Sai up and rushed under a tree, which provided little cover. She held Sai close to her, very tight. He cried for a while and then went to sleep. It had started raining heavily and Vidya swiftly moved towards a closed shop; it would provide better protection. She did not want to go far as Amma would be back soon. She shivered in the wet cold, but she held on to Sai. She wanted to give him as much heat as possible. It must have been hours and she dozed off.

She was woken up in the morning by the shopkeeper.

"Wake up, girl. Who are you?"

"Vidya."

"What are you doing here?"

"Waiting for Amma," replied Vidya in all innocence. "She has not come back yet."

"Ok, come sit in the corner here."

It had stopped raining and the night had passed. Amma had still not come.

"Sai, get up."

Sai did not get up.

"Sai?" her voice was trembling.

The shopkeeper rushed to check.

"Who is he?"

"My brother, Sai"

The shopkeeper tried rubbing Sai's cold feet and hands as Vidya stepped back and watched with horror written all over her face.

"What happened, uncle? Why is Sai not getting up?"

People had gathered by then. Vidya touched Sai's tiny hands. They were much too cold. The horribly familiar realisation swept over Vidya again – Sai was no more. Vidya wailed, crying for Amma. She did not want to leave. She was waiting for Amma. Amma had gone to get medicine and left little Sai in her care. What would she say to Amma now? She had not taken care of Sai. Sai, her little brother. Sai, her life.

Amma did not come back. Vidya was lost, frantic with despair and hopelessness when she saw the old lady on the temple steps. She ran towards her.

"Aunty, where is Amma?'

"Whose Amma?"

"My Amma. You took her to Gangu yesterday. You said you would get her new work. She has not come back and Sai . . . He . . . He's . . ." Vidya ran out of breath, couldn't get the words out.

The old lady's voice softened. "Oh, that's bad. A lot of bad things have happened to you, dear. Your Amma should have come back by now. Come, let us go check with Gangu. She went to check for a new job."

'But Sai?"

"Yes. Sai. Ok, you stay here, let me see." The old woman walked away limping.

Gangu came to meet Vidya for the first time. He was stout, dark and shabbily dressed. A few men followed him everywhere. He had big eyes. Big, red eyes. Vidya was crying. Gangu came up to Vidya and sat down beside her. He patted her gently.

"So, you are Punnamma's daughter?"

"Yes. Do you know where she is?"

"No. She came to meet me yesterday, but I did not have any new work for her. I asked her to go back to her children. God knows where she went."

Vidya started crying again. She was scared. She felt so alone in the big bad world, scared of everything around her.

"Let us wait for some more time. I'm sure she will come back."

Minutes turned to hours and there was no news of Amma. Vidya was helpless. She clung to Sai's cold body. She did not want to let go of him. She still hoped he would get up, that he would cry, he would smile. She desperately wanted Sai to be alright.

"Sai, please get up. I won't be angry if you cry again. Just get up. Please get up." Her voice trailed off.

"We can't keep the body near the temple like this," objected somebody.

"True, we can't do that," said another voice.

Vidya's hold tightened.

"What happened?" asked a lady who'd been drawn by the crowd.

"This girl's brother died in the rains yesterday, and her mother has abandoned them."

"She must have run away with someone leaving the poor kids on the temple steps."

"God! How can a mother do something so horrible?"

There were many more stories.

"How can Amma abandon us?"

Vidya's innocent mind was being poisoned. Tired, hungry, desperate, she no longer knew what truth was – she'd been left alone. Amma said she'd come back. She didn't. She'd left Vidya and Sai all alone, and now all she had was Sai's tiny, limp, lifeless body. She was angry

– how could Amma do this! She'd promised to come back. Promised!

The police arrived soon. Statements were taken. Statements from strangers, people Vidya had never seen before, passersby. Vidya was also questioned and all she could say was, "Amma went for work and did not come back."

Towards evening, the dreaded Municipality came again and took Sai this time. Vidya did not want to cremate her little brother, but was made to do so much against her will. When you have nothing, your will can't do much.

CHAPTER 23

Angel's Evil Guardian

Gangu came to meet her that evening. "Child, I know what you are going through, but you need not fear. I am here for you. I will take care of you."

Vidya looked at him blankly. She did not know what to do. What choice did she have? There was nobody else to turn to, nobody else offering any help. She was vulnerable. She sobbed as if her body would be torn apart.

Turning to the old woman, Gangu continued "You, you better take good care of the girl. I will keep checking on her."

The old woman nodded. They exchanged glances that conveyed some message Vidya could not understand. Then, with a gentle smile, Gangu patted Vidya and tried to console her.

"Look darling, I've been searching for your mother since morning. I will let you know about her as soon as I find out. You just stay here. Take care."

Gangu sat there speaking to Vidya for about half hour before he left. Vidya could not sleep that night. Whenever she dozed off, she dreamt of Sai, of Nana. She dreamt of Amma running away and she ran after her, trying to stop her, pleading with her to come back. She would wake up with a start, start crying until she dozed off again.

In the past few days she had heard so much about her mother that she no longer knew what she believed. People told different stories.

"My mother is not like that," she would tell herself. "These people have never met Amma, how can they say that?"

There was conflict in her mind. Her heart was not ready to believe that her mother had abandoned her and had left Sai to die, but evidence suggested otherwise. Gangu took good care of her, brought her toys, but she seemed to have lost interest in everything. She did not want to play with the other street urchins. She withdrew from the crowd and seldom smiled. She sat in a corner staring at people, her eyes still searching for Amma. Gangu would come and spend some time with her each evening, telling her stories and jokes to make her smile. Although she was not a fun-loving child anymore, she started trusting Gangu. After all, made sure she was fed and seemed to care about her. He was the only one who did.

CHAPTER 24

The Ultimate Betrayal

The sun was just setting when Gangu came with the old lady. Vidya had not found out her name yet. She did not care to ask, either. Gangu smiled at her warmly while the old lady stood there, stooped and leaning on the stick in her hand.

"How's the little girl today?" Gangu's voice was cheerful.

Vidya did not respond.

"Here, see what I brought for you." Gangu put his hands in his pocket. His pants really needed a wash. He held out his hand with orange candies in them. Vidya looked at them and then looked away.

"Dear, I have some news for you" Gangu said. He did not force Vidya to have the candies. He knew she would not take them.

"What?"

"We've found out where your mother is."

For the first time in so many days, there was hope in Vidya's eyes.

"Where? Where is Amma? Please take me to her." She sounded impatient.

"I wish we could take you there, but it is not a good place."

"I don't care. Where is Amma?"

"She is with the police."

The old lady stood there silently.

"With the police? Why? What did she do?" Vidya was scared again. "How do you know about her?"

"I met her today. I told her about you and your brother." He paused watching Vidya's expressions very closely. "She did not seem to care. Darling, she has indeed abandoned you."

"No. It cannot be true. I don't trust you. Take me to her. The police are bad. Take me to her."

"Ok. Ok. I will take you to meet her, but what if the police catch you too?"

"But why did they catch Amma?"

This time, the old lady spoke. "She was caught by the police for doing the wrong things."

"Wrong things? What wrong things?"

"She was caught along with many other ladies in a brothel."

"What is that?"

"Bad place; not for good girls."

"Why did Amma go there?"

The old lady did not say anything except to repeat, "God help you, God save you."

Vidya was quiet. She had seen a movie in her village where the bad girls sang and danced in front of men, who gave them lots of money. Men who smoked and drank. They were bad girls, very bad girls. But why had Amma become bad?

Her thoughts were broken by the old lady's words who seemed to be choosing her words carefully. She was speaking to Gangu. "God, we can never trust anyone. Her mother seemed a nice lady. A mother of two little angels. How much her husband must have loved her! He wasn't dead longer than a few days and she goes to other men. Why did she not think of her kids even once?"

There was more melodrama as the lady cried aloud. Vidya cried as well.

Gangu stroked Vidya lovingly. "She really is an angel. So innocent and so pure. I will take care of you, my love. I will make sure you are safe."

The trick seemed to be working. Vidya could feel resentment against her mother filling her. Yes, she was the cause of all misery, she was the cause of Sai's death. She had left her children and run away. She did not stop the Municipality when they took Nana. Vidya's heart had been full of pain, but now that pain was turning into hatred. It was evident on her face although she did not speak. Gangu and the old lady exchanged glances and smiled slyly.

"Come child, you cannot stay on the streets forever with the stray dogs. Let me take you to a place where there are many more children like you," Gangu said.

Vidya did not move.

"You will like the place dear. You will be safe. You will be taken care of." Saying so, Gangu held Vidya's hand and pulled. Vidya got up.

"My money?" The old lady asked.

"You've got enough." Gangu raised his voice in anger.

"But it's just . . ."

"It was because of your foolishness and drunkenness that I suffered the loss. You should have been with the child that night. You've got enough for one."

The old lady seemed to understand since she nodded her head, but Vidya did not. Not then, not until much later when she realised the web of deceit that had been laid out for Amma, herself and for Sai. Unfortunately, Sai was the loss Gangu spoke about.

CHAPTER 25

Broken Trust

Vidya was taken to an orphanage where there were many children; some her age, a few older and a few small babies. Vidya looked around warily.

"Come darling, this is a home for children. See there are so many around here, laughing and playing. You will love their company." Gangu walked towards the entrance.

"Aah! See who comes here!" a middle-aged woman exclaimed, approaching them with a smile.

"Vidya, this is Kamala. She is the guardian here. All children are under her care. She is very sweet, she will love you."

Vidya tried to hide behind Gangu.

"Oh! What a pretty little girl! So, this is Vidya." Kamala smiled as she looked at the little girl.

"Yes. And you better take good care of her."

"Gangu, I don't want to be here."

"Darling, you'll be fine here with all other children. See, look how happy they are" Gangu pointed towards the little children playing on the swings.

The children did indeed seem happy. They were running around, noisy and laughing, but Vidya was not comfortable.

"I'll come to meet you now and then."

"Come, child, let me introduce you to some of your new friends." Kamla led the hesitant Vidya into the corridor.

"Rupa, Savitri," Kamla called out as two girls of about Vidya's age came running. Their hair was unkempt but their clothes were washed. There was innocence in their naughty eyes and smiles on their faces.

"Come here, girls; meet Vidya, she's new here." The girls smiled at Vidya. Vidya smiled back nervously.

"Come on, take her along and go play. Make sure she settles in well and makes friends," Gangu told the girls as they held Vidya's hand and led her away.

Vidya kept turning back to look at Gangu again and again. Gangu smiled at her, waving to her before walking away into with Kamala, closing the door behind him. That was the last she ever saw of Gangu.

As the sun set, the bell rang and all children assembled in the long corridor where they were made to sit on the cold floor and served rice and curry, which they ate hungrily. It had been a long time since Vidya last ate something well cooked. She remembered the meals she'd had with her family. There was a lump in her throat as the memories welled up and she could hardly swallow the food. She slept on the mat with the rest of the kids and was woken up by another bell in the morning.

Rupa was dusky and frail, and had the most beautiful smile. "We need to take bath and assemble for prayers before breakfast," she explained. Vidya nodded and followed her.

Vidya made friends easily and days seemed to pass without incident. But it was not in Vidya's fate to settle down. Not so soon. Not so easily.

CHAPTER 26

Mr. & Mrs. Thomas

It was a Sunday, and the morning was bright and sunny. It had drizzled at night and the sweet smell of wet earth still lingered in the air. Sparrows chirped as the bell rang and the children in the orphanage got up lazily. Vidya wanted to sleep a little longer, but there were rules to follow. She had started to smile again, but the pain in her life was still apparent. She brushed her teeth still half asleep and had her bath. After prayers and breakfast of two idlis, she was summoned by Kamala.

She entered the small, dingy room, which was supposed to be the office. There was an old wooden table in the centre, where Kamala sat. There were two more vacant tin chairs of tin. The only light in the room filtered in through the only window behind where Kamala sat. A pungent smell filled the air. The walls needed to be whitewashed, but the floor had been swept and mopped. Kamala was wearing a crisp cotton saree with a contrast border as she usually did. Her hair was tied neatly in a bun. The scent of the fresh white mogra flowers which she tied over her bun could be sensed even in the overpowering dampness of the room.

"Ah, Vidya, come in, dear," Kamala greeted her warmly, smiling. "Come, come close to me," she continued pulling Vidya gently towards her. "Good, you seem to have had a nice bath. You smell fresh!"

Vidya stood still.

"Here darling, I have some new clothes for you." Kamala opened a draw in the table and held out a brown paper packet.

"Come on! Open it and see."

Vidya extended her hand to take the packet.

"Go on, open it up."

There was a beautiful baby pink frock with bright blue flowers and ribbons to match.

"Do you like it?"

Vidya nodded.

"Here, I have something else for you," said Kamala, handing her another packet.

Vidya opened it to find a pair of socks and shoes. She looked at Kamala questioningly.

"These are also for you. Now go along with *ayah* and get dressed soon."

"Get dressed?" Vidya asked, confused. "What for?"

"You dress up and come. I will tell you then." There was excitement in Kamala's voice. "You are a lucky girl. You really are."

Vidya was led away by the ayah who dressed her. Her long tresses were neatly combed, plaited and tied with the beautiful ribbons. The ayah also placed white mogra flowers in her hair and made her wear socks and shoes. Vidya had never worn shoes before. Her feet felt caged.

"Ayah, can I wear my slippers please, my feet feel jailed in these shoes."

Ayah laughed aloud at Vidya's innocent expression. "They will be fine. You look so beautiful. Just like a princess. Come, let's go now."

Kamala inspected Vidya. She seemed satisfied. There was a smile of contentment on her face, like a cat full of cream.

"Come girl, sit here," she said, pointing towards the chair.

Vidya sat down hesitantly.

"Now listen very carefully to me." Vidya looked up at her.

"There is a couple from a good family coming down to our orphanage today. I want you to behave your best." Vidya did not understand why she was being briefed.

"They are from a very good family, very rich. They will ask you few questions." She paused. "Make sure you answer them with a smile." She looked at Vidya as though trying to read her.

"You will, Vidya, won't you?"

Vidya nodded again. "But why will they ask me questions? What will they ask me?"

"Oh! Nothing. Nothing much. Just a few things about you."

"About me?" Vidya was surprised.

"Yes about you. They are coming to meet you, and if they like you, your life will be made, girl! Your life will be made!" Kamala could not hide the excitement in her voice. "They will also donate a good amount of money to our orphanage."

There was a loud horn outside as a black Ambassador car drove in. Kamala moved swiftly towards the door to peep.

"Here they come. Ayah, take Vidya with you. Bring her only when I call," she said, rushing out as Vidya was led back inside the orphanage.

Vidya's heart raced. Once inside the room, she gathered courage and asked "Ayah, what's all this? I do not understand."

"Why are you so upset? Smile. There are other children also dressed up like you for those people."

"Then why was I called by Kamala?"

"Because it's your first time meeting the guests."

"Oh, so they are guests. I understand."

Ayah smiled and didn't say a word. No one wanted a scene at this time. After about 15 minutes they heard Kamala call out.

"Come, dear, remember to smile and wish the guests."

"Yes. I will. We also had guests all the time in our village." Vidya said somewhat enthusiastically. She liked her new clothes. She smiled naturally for the first time in a long while.

Vidya was led by the ayah into the office once again.

Dressed in a short-sleeved jacket with a peplum and a full skirt, a string of freshwater pearl necklace and poodle-cut hair sat a very beautiful, elegant lady with blue eyes. Her red painted lips parted into a smile on seeing Vidya, showing pearly-white teeth. Beside her was an equally handsome, broad-shouldered man in single-breasted two-piece suit with wet-look hair parted on the side. Vidya was amused. They seemed to have popped right out of Thaatha's stories. She always thought fairies lived high up above the clouds.

"This is Vidya." Kamala introduced them to the couple. "And Vidya, this is Mrs. and Mr. Thomas. They're from England. Say hello!"

Vidya folded her hands and said, "*Namaste.*"

Mrs. and Mr. Thomas smiled warmly and replied, "Namaste."

Their voices sounded strange to Vidya. "Oh, she's so beautiful! Come here, darling!"

Mrs. Thomas got up and came close to Vidya. They spoke English and Vidya could hardly understand a word or two. She smiled shyly. Mr. Thomas also got up and came close. He patted Vidya gently.

"I think I'm in love with this angel."

"Yes, she's so good and so innocent. Just look at her bright eyes and smile."

Kamala and Ayah smiled with joy as Mr. Thomas took out a piece of candy from his pocket and offered it to Vidya. Vidya looked at Kamala who immediately said, "Take it child. It's for you." Vidya hesitated for a while and then took the candy.

Mrs. Thomas was delighted. It was evident from her voice and her actions. She asked Vidya to sit beside her. There was a conversation in English. Kamala did not speak very fluent English like Mrs. and Mr. Thomas did, but she managed. She made gestures with her hands, raised her eyes, as if to express something very dramatic. She was definitely saying something about Vidya, because every now and then she paused to let Mrs. Thomas ruffle Vidya's hair and wipe her tears with her handkerchief. Mr. Thomas appeared equally moved. He bent forward to gently kiss Vidya's forehead. Vidya sat there looking at Kamala, trying to make out what she was explaining. She looked at Mrs. and Mr. Thomas – now they looked sad. Why were they being so affectionate towards her? It all felt like a puzzle to Vidya, and she tried to solve it, but couldn't understand. She had been to school in the village, but that was more than a year ago. She had forgotten most of what she had learnt, but words like 'poor child, mother, father, dead, very sad' seemed familiar. She tried putting these pieces together and then realised that Kamala was briefing Mrs. and Mr. Thomas about her, and they were touched by her heart-breaking story.

"But how does Kamala know so much about me?" she thought, and answered her own question "Okay, Gangu must have told her. But why is she telling it to these people?" Vidya was lost in her own thoughts as Kamala continued.

Hot tea and biscuits were served. Mrs. Thomas offered a biscuit to Vidya, who still had the candy in her hand. She shook her head.

"Don't be shy Vidya. Have the biscuits." But Vidya did not want to have anything. She looked at Kamala and bent her head down.

"It's okay, don't push her," said Mr. Thomas in his thick and masculine voice, which was surprisingly gentle.

"Sir, you can have tea, it is ginger masala tea." Kamala offered a cup to Mr. Thomas.

"Thank you so much. But we would like to have lunch with Vidya at home."

"Oh yes. I'm so excited. You'll come along with Mommy, won't you?" Mrs. Thomas's voice was filled with happiness and excitement.

"Of course she will," replied Kamala.

"Good. Then we sign the papers. I want everything smooth and legal."

"Yes. Yes, of course! Everything is legal here. This orphanage is approved by the government," Kamala pointed towards a framed certificate on the wall. "You can have a look at it yourself," she continued, walking towards the wall. "This man here with me in the picture is the Mantriji. You don't need to worry about anything." She walked back to her desk and pulled out some old files from it. "Here, take a look at these. You can satisfy yourself thoroughly."

Mr. Thomas flipped through a few papers. "These seem to be quite old."

"Yes. We keep a record of everything. We have new files there as well." She pointed towards an old cupboard.

Then, pulling out a big bunch of keys she called to the ayah, "Take out a few files and show Mr. Thomas."

"Yes, Madam."

While taking the keys Vidya noticed that they exchanged glances, conveying some message. Ayah moved towards the cupboard and then pulled out files. She carried more files than she could in her hand, and when she came near the table, she dropped all of them. It was obviously staged, but the couple were so engaged with Vidya that they did not notice the studied deliberation of the act.

"Oh nonsense! You can never do one thing right. Now pick up those files quick," reprimanded Kamala.

Ayah bent to pick up the files and jumbled most of them up. She then placed the pile on the table and excused herself in a hurry.

"Oh Lord, now it will take ages to put this in order."

"What do we do now? We can't sit here forever and sort through these files." Mrs. Thomas spoke.

"I'm sorry. Let's do one thing. Our *wakil* will come down to your guesthouse tomorrow first thing in the morning. I will send a few papers for you. You can check them and give your approval."

"Oh no, I wanted to take the child home with me today."

"Yes, sweetheart, but we need to make sure the papers are in order as well," said Mr. Thomas, who seemed bent on doing things right.

"I was thinking of buying her presents on our way back." Mrs. Thomas was evidently very disappointed.

"Sir, you can fill the form and rest assured. You can take the child with you. I promise there will be no cause for worry. Our lawyer will also make the other documents in a few days, proper government documents, all legal."

"Please, love," Mrs. Thomas pleaded.

"Alright. But if anything is not up to my satisfaction . . ."

"You will not have any reason for complaint!" Kamala did not let Mr. Thomas complete his sentence.

"Does the child know?" he asked.

"Not yet. I will explain it to her. She is a smart girl."

It was then that Vidya came to know what was going on, but there wasn't much she could do. She was a puppet and danced as the strings were pulled by hands and fingers that had decided the choreography of her life.

Chapter 27

Search For The Dead

Now Vidya had a new home—a new family with a new Mom and Dad.

"God! I always asked you for new clothes, new toys, new shoes. But new family with new parents?" She felt like the one piece of a puzzle which did not want to fit in to complete the picture. She did not like it. Not a bit.

There were big smiles on faces of Mr. and Mrs. Thomas as they gently held Vidya's hands at the airport. All formalities were over. All papers were ready. Vidya was officially adopted with a new name: Vidya Thomas. As they entered the airport, Mrs. Thomas gently held Vidya's little fingers. Vidya was nervous. She followed the couple, silently waiting for her turn in the queue. They cleared security and sat at the lounge. Through the big glass windows, Vidya saw the huge aeroplanes. One taxied towards the runway before taking off. Vidya was astounded. She saw people climbing the stairs and getting into one of the giant structures before the doors closed. Her eyes were wide open, as was her mouth.

Mr. Thomas laughed gently, and then coming close to Vidya, tried to explain with elaborate gestures. "That's an aeroplane." He said pointing out to one on the tarmac. He then pointed towards Vidya, himself and Mrs. Thomas. "We will all fly in that".

His palms pointed towards the sky. Vidya looked at him, then at the aeroplane and then at the sky and then at Mr. Thomas again. Ruffling her hair he pulled her closer. "Don't worry, we are with you."

Vidya seemed to understand what was being conveyed. There was an announcement as all passengers got up and slowly moved towards the door that led them towards the aeroplane. Vidya was hesitant. She had to be coaxed. Mr. Thomas's gentle smile was reassuring. She held his hand tightly. Mrs. Thomas bent down to plant a gentle kiss on her forehead, but Vidya moved away swiftly. The couple had noticed that Vidya was receptive to Mr. Thomas, but distanced herself from Mrs. Thomas, which was quite the opposite of what they had expected.

"It's fine. We need to give her time to adjust to her new life. I am sure, she will take to you soon," Mr. Thomas assured his worried wife, who took a deep breath and nodded understandingly before heading towards the exit.

Vidya sat in the window seat next to her new father. She looked around anxiously as the air hostesses helped the passengers stash their bags away. There was an announcement and Mr. Thomas secured Vidya's seat belt as the plane started taxiing before taking off. Vidya held her breath and Mr. Thomas gently placed his big hands on her small ones, smiling warmly. Vidya got little comfort as she shut her eyes tight and clenched her fists. She could feel a strange sensation in her stomach. She was terrified. A few scary minutes later, when they were up in the sky and the strange feeling eased, Vidya opened her eyes. Vidya peeped down to see the ground below. It reminded her of the time when she and her family were airlifted after the storm that had shattered her life forever. She could feel the pain in her fragile chest as it brought back memories of her beloved Thaatha, Nana and Sai.

As the plane rose, she could see the clouds float. Soft as cotton balls, they drifted all around. All of a sudden Vidya was alert, and she peeped out of the little window as though searching for something.

"All departed souls live in heaven. Up, up in the skies, on the soft floating clouds, they fly and keep a watch on their loved ones below." She had heard tales of fairies, of heaven, of the loved ones becoming stars; and now she was flying in the midst of the clouds, in the sky.

"Heaven has to be here, somewhere here; and if it's so, Thaatha, Nana and Sai will be there." Vidya wiped her tears away – they blurred her vision. She did not wish to miss the moment. Her heart throbbed painfully.

"Darling, have a sip." Mrs. Thomas's voice brought her back, as a pretty airhostess smiled at her, offering her a glass of orange juice. Vidya did not want to be disturbed or distracted. She gulped it down hurriedly and was back peeping through the thick glass window, her eyes wide open. If she could've helped it, she wouldn't have blinked. The world below looked so tiny, the huge hills and mountains looked as small as ice cream cones. She could hardly make out the shapes of houses below. Men and women must be the size of ants, she thought.

"How can Nana find me from here?" There were so many questions storming her little mind, and then there was huge body of water. Oh, good God! So much of water on earth? It seemed endless. She shuddered as she kept peeping out into the sky.

"Wake up, love, the plane is about to land." Vidya woke up with a jerk. She found herself curled up on Mr. Thomas's lap.

"When did I go to sleep? Why did you not wake me up?" Her eyes were wet again as she peeped out of the window.

The land below was clearly visible now. The roads, buildings and grasslands were all closing in fast and the clouds and the sky were going farther away. Vidya cursed herself. How could she have fallen asleep? How could she? Nana, Thaatha and Sai would have come, and she was sleeping?

"Why did you let me sleep?" she almost accused Mr. and Mrs. Thomas as though it was their fault.

They smiled at her comfortingly as Mrs. Thomas tried to wipe her tears away with the warm white towel offered on the plane. Vidya turned her face away, wiping her tears with her small fingers. They could not understand what she said, but they knew she was in pain and it pained them too. It was going to be a very rough road ahead, and they would have to invest their energy in making the journey as smooth as possible.

A few minutes after the landing announcement, the plane touched ground and a cool gust of breeze and clear skies welcomed Vidya as she stepped out of the plane onto the land which would be her new home.

CHAPTER 28

A New Beginning

Vidya quietly followed the couple through the airport and all the formalities, and into a chauffeured Morris Minor 4-seater. It was a pleasant evening and everything seemed beautiful. The roads were broad and clean lined with trees in full bloom. Vidya had never seen such a beautiful city. It was like a fairyland and she was mesmerised. For a moment she forgot all her pain and peeped out of the car. Men and women here were so different from where she had come. Their attire, skin, hair and the way they carried themselves, not to mention their language, were all so different. As the car took a turn at the roundabout, she was amazed to see beautiful houses, big, palatial buildings with glass windows covered by gauzy white curtains. Every house had a small garden in front with colourful flowers, and a car parked in front. The sky was clear and beautiful with clouds like cotton candy floating above. Vidya took a deep breath in the cool breeze as though soaking up the atmosphere. Another turn and the car came to a halt at the cul-de-sac in front of a detached house on slightly raised ground. Mrs. and Mr. Thomas got out. Vidya followed very hesitantly.

The door was opened by a young woman who seemed to be the housekeeper. She set her foot on the oak flooring with a beautiful rug.

Mrs. Thomas smiled at her. "Welcome home, Princess!" she exclaimed.

Vidya could understand that much. She had been to school and she did understand some English. She smiled nervously as Mr. Thomas led her towards the plush sofa and sat her down. Vidya explored the vast hallway silently with her eyes. There were huge glass-panelled doors and walk-in closets. She was then led into the luxurious living room. At the centre of the stone wall was the fireplace, flanked by bookshelves. Vidya had loved books, but she had not seen such a huge collection ever before, not even in her old school. There was a big framed painting adorning the giant room. She looked up to see the ornate ceiling and the beautiful chandelier. The large oak trees outside stood majestically like sentinels. Beyond them was a thicket.

Vidya had come from a small village and a humble dwelling where the thatched roof was repaired every year before the rains. The lime and mortar walls were just high enough for the men to stand upright. Candles and lanterns illuminated the huts every evening, which were blown out before the family called it a day. Vidya could never have imagined such opulence!

"Yes, darling, you want to say something?"

Vidya shook her head.

"Alright, do you need something?"

She shook her head again.

Mr. Thomas sat beside her as the housekeeper brought in glasses of fresh juice. Handing Vidya a glass, he said very slowly, "This is now *your* home." Pausing so that the little one could understand, he continued, *"We are now a family."*

Vidya understood, but she could not agree. How could complete strangers just walk into her shattered life and be family? Her family was no more. Nana and Sai were dead and her mother had abandoned her. She was all alone. How could she trust anyone? She quietly sipped the orange juice, holding the delicately carved glass tightly, afraid that it would slip out of her small hands and break.

Mrs. Thomas took her up the staircase to a room with big Venetian windows. A queen-sized bed with white linen and a colourful quilt was in the centre, with big pillows and bright throw cushions. There was a big wardrobe and a door beside it opened into a fascinating bathroom, complete with a bath tub. The grandeur of every corner mesmerised young Vidya, but offered no comfort.

A young lady walked into the room. She must have been in her early twenties, fair with golden hair, blue eyes and an enchanting smile.

"This is Ann," Mrs. Thomas introduced her. "She will be taking care of you."

Vidya looked at Ann. She was confused. Why did anyone have to take care of her? And how would Ann take care of her?

As though she'd read the thoughts frantically flitting through her mind, Ann bent down and with the most charming smile gently said, "I will teach you everything"

"Teacher?"

Ann laughed "No, no, I'm your friend. I will play with you, tell you stories, and take care of you. But first, let us just go in and have some fun with water."

Vidya resisted. She hated water. It was the cause of her misery.

Ann smiled and held her hand gently leading her in the bath tub filled warm water. "You will feel fresh, and then tomorrow we will go shopping and buy you some goodies. There are big parks around here with lots of swings. We will have loads of fun." Ann lifted Vidya and placed her in the bathtub.

Vidya did indeed feel good. There wasn't so much water that she would drown and warmth felt wonderful to her tired body. There was something nice about Ann. Vidya thought she might like her.

The bath was refreshing, and Vidya felt very light. Although she had slept during the flight, she felt sleepy again, but Ann made sure Vidya had a bowl of hot soup before that.

"Yes, darling, you want to ask something?"

Vidya nodded "Thomas . . . ."

"Yes, Mr. and Mrs Thomas?"

She nodded again and questioned, "King?"

Ann laughed again. "No. Why do you ask?"

Looking all around the little girl struggled to explain "Big house. Good bed. Car," she said, hesitantly.

"They are now your parents. And you definitely are a princess! Now, off to bed."

It did not take long for Vidya to doze off.

Thus began Vidya's new journey where Ann did become more of a friend and confidante as she groomed and schooled the young girl in the ways of the new world. Bedtime stories from folklore were now replaced by Cinderella and Goldilocks. She loved listening to stories of Snow White and her adventures with the Seven Dwarfs, Alice's trip down the rabbit hole to Wonderland and the Sleeping Beauty's happy ending as much as she had loved the stories narrated by Nana from the **Ramayana** and **Mahabharata**.

CHAPTER 29

Colossus

The Thomases were rich, and now were blessed with Vidya as their daughter. They were happy that their family was now complete. Mr. Thomas's business was spread across many countries. He had made his way in the world the hard way. He'd never been to college. Before he found success, each day had been a struggle, and bread and butter had been a luxury. Mr Thomas had lost his father when he was just a boy. His mother was a simple woman who struggled to make ends meet. As a teenager, he'd been acutely aware of his mother's predicament. He loved his mother and hated to see her slog day and night to fill their bellies. He dropped out of school and sought a job as a cleaner on board *Colossus*. It was a huge cargo vessel that sailed across many oceans and countries. It was as strong and as impressive as its name indicated. It was one of the most admired vessels of its time. Being a part of *Colossus* was something to be proud of. Many of his young friends had envied him. The young man had been overjoyed at the idea of travelling around the world. It was his very first tryst with freedom and responsibility.

It was here that he had met Ying, a Chinese trader, known for his Midas touch. Very rich and powerful, he was equally known and respected for his wisdom and business acumen. He was small, kind and humble—a wise man who knew in which baskets to place his eggs.

When the young Thomas first saw Ying, he wondered if Ying was truly deserving of the reverence and honour commanded. He sat on the deck, gorging on the **Dim Sum** and **Chow Fun**. He was unassumingly simple for such a wealthy man. One would have expected the young tycoon to be dressed in a business suit with smart touches that elegantly but discreetly proclaimed his wealth. But here Ying sat on a simple wooden chair enjoying his simple meal. There were no airs about him.

When Ying was done, Thomas went up to clean the table. Ying smiled at him and Thomas smiled back nervously. "What's your name young man? Not seen you around here."

"Carlson Thomas. I am new here."

Ying nodded his head as he rinsed his fingers. "Have you worked on the vessels before?"

"No sir, this is my first job. I do not have any experience, but I work hard, I assure you of that," Thomas had replied confidently.

Ying smiled. "You are young, why did you take up this job? You know it will be months before we come back to England again."

"I am well aware and prepared, Mr. Ying. I would like to travel the globe and gain rich experience in your company. It is an honour to be aboard **Colossus**."

"Hmmmm," Ying went on to sip his tea as the fresh sea breeze blew.

Thomas had not expected such an interaction with his employer. It was a pleasant surprise. "That's what makes him the man he is," said Larry joining him in the ship's kitchen. "He knows us all by name, treats us like family."

Young Thomas was impressed by Mr. Ying. He learned a lot from his simplicity and modesty. Mr. Ying was a true businessman when it came to matters of the trade. He bargained fiercely and got his deals on his own terms.

"Your product should be the best, the finest. Nothing less than that would do, and then you need to be able to read the trends of the market, ready to capitalise on the dents to demand your price," he once told the inquisitive Thomas.

Colossus sailed through oceans to far off countries like Russia, Columbia, England, India and many more countries, leaving behind its legacy as it cruised ahead.

Mr. Ying was passionate about business and he saw the same spark in Thomas. "You will do good business," he once told Thomas. "Mark my words, you will."

Young Thomas was enterprising. He quickly learned the intricacies of trade and soon started trading silk with small merchants from China and India. He weathered all the storms that came his way, and his charm, hard work and the business sense he had learned from Mr. Ying proved very useful. Slowly and steadily he expanded his business.

When Mr. Thomas was honoured with the "Businessman of the Year" award, he did not forget to mention his Mr Ying.

CHAPTER 30

Friends And Fairy Tales

Business meetings and trips kept Mr. Thomas busy, but he made sure that Vidya was well taken care of, went to the best school, brought her gifts from all over the world. Mr. Thomas gained her trust. She would often sit beside him and hold his hand as he told her stories, shared jokes and took her out fishing, cycling, hiking and camping. She loved adventures and Mr. Thomas made sure she had fun during her vacations. He pampered and spoiled her silly. Vidya would make lovely, hand-painted cards and present them to her Dad every Father's Day.

Mrs. Thomas stayed at home, made the best cookies and baked cakes for Vidya. She tried hard to get close to her, spend as much time as possible, but there seemed to be a distance between them that she couldn't bridge. Something that held Vidya back, not letting her accept Mrs. Thomas as her mother. She seldom gave her a loving smile, which hurt Mrs. Thomas, but she bore it with grace and dignity.

Vidya had always been a bright girl. It did not take her long to settle down and adapt to the new country and culture. But her past never left her in peace. Her mother's betrayal stayed with her like a bitter poison. She hated to be ordered, making her rebel of sorts. As she grew older, the struggle became intense. She had always been buffeted by the winds of fate. She wanted to be in control. She wanted to take the reins of her destiny in her own hands, but life always had different plans for her.

It took time, but Vidya made friends and was quite popular in her school. She was a good student, academically as well as in other activities. She excelled in sports, took part in plays, learnt to dance and played the violin like a pro. She was undoubtedly talented, but she had mood swings and trusted slowly and seldom.

Her friends were interested in her stories, some of which she had heard from Nana. She remembered a few of them. They were amused by how Vidya used to travel by bullock carts. They believed her story when she told with pride that her Nana could punch a tiger. She loved the attention.

"Did you have a snake for a pet?" asked one of her friends.

"Oh no, but we had Bheema, Lakshmi and Gauri."

"Did you stay in the jungle?" they asked.

"No, no, we had our house. Our own house in the village." She described her hut and the tamarind and mango trees outside.

"So you come from the prehistoric age?"

Vidya could not explain the unfairness of the disparity that existed in the world, nor could her little friends understand.

Vidya loved the English stories where a little girl was lost in wonderland, the pumpkin turned into a chariot at the stroke of midnight and the bears could have porridge for breakfast. They were so different from the ones she heard from Nana.

"Who could have taught the animals to cook?" She thought.

On bright sunny summer holidays, children would get together and venture into the woods close by. They picked berries and wandered around the woods, imagining themselves to be characters from their bedtime stories. Mr. Thomas had also made a tree house where she and her friends spent most of the afternoons.

CHAPTER 31

It Is What You Choose

One day, Vidya came home from school tense and wound up taut as a spring. It was weekend, but she chose to stay indoors. She shut her door and lay on the bed with her shoes still on.

"Vidya looks worried, why don't you find out what the matter is, Ann?" Mrs. Thomas was worried.

"Yeah, I noticed." Taking a can of juice and a sandwich, Ann knocked on the door.

"Who's that?" Vidya sounded annoyed.

"It's me," Ann replied.

"Alright, come in," Vidya let Ann in reluctantly. She could not say no to Ann.

"What's it dear? You look worried."

"Yeah, sure I am. That *goddamn* teacher gave my name for the debate, knowing very well how I hate those competitions."

"I'm sure she knows what you are capable of!"

"Sure she does! I can hardly stammer on stage. There were others who were dying to be a picked, but she chose me! Would you believe it? She chose me!" she continued, angry and frustrated.

"And do you know the topic?"

"You tell me."

"Of Thorns and Roses, it's what you choose."

"That's an interesting topic!"

"You bet, as interesting as a melting ice-cream cone!"

Ann laughed aloud at the comparison.

"Ann, stop laughing. I seriously don't want to be a part of it."

"You already are, my dear!"

"Yeah I know, so do something. Help me out. I don't want to be made a laughing stock," pleaded Vidya.

"Come on Vidya, you are better than you think you are! I am sure you will be good."

"Isn't there a way out?"

"No. Absolutely not. In fact, I think it's your chance and you should grab it!"

"Fine, then, you can very well help me prepare!"

Ann took a deep breath, "I wish I could, but you know that I am going home this weekend. I have already promised them."

"I'm doomed, then!" Vidya said, dramatically.

"Of course not, you have Mrs. Thomas with you and she will be more than happy to help you out!"

Vidya shook her head and screwed up her nose as she slumped on the bed again.

With Mr. Thomas on a business trip and Ann leaving for the weekend, Vidya had no choice. She could either be a butt of the jokes of the envious few who wished they were in her shoes, or walk up to Mrs. Thomas, who indeed was delighted at the request.

Mother and daughter spent hours perfecting the opening speech and the possible rebuttals. They butted heads quite often as Vidya had her own opinion of life and Mrs. Thomas was trying to explain the essence of the subject. Vidya argued vehemently and Mrs. Thomas had the patience of a saint.

"I give up; we never seem to agree on anything, so let's just get it over with." Vidya walked out in a huff carrying the paper in her hand.

It was a very nervous Monday morning as Vidya got dressed for school.

"Darling! You need not follow all my suggestions today. It is about your thoughts and your opinion! You can voice them. It's your views and I'm sure of your capabilities," Mrs. Thomas said as she wished Vidya good luck.

Vidya walked out without a word.

That evening, Ann was back and opened the door as Vidya rushed in excitedly. She held the trophy in her hands. She was jumping with joy.

"Ann! Would you believe, I won! I won!"

"Congratulations! That's awesome!" Ann hugged Vidya.

Vidya kissed her trophy again and again. She could not believe that she'd done it. She ran and grabbed the telephone and dialled a number.

"Dad! I won the trophy! I won the trophy!" Vidya could not contain her happiness. "My friends could not believe it! My teacher was so proud of me!" Vidya was thrilled as she described her victory to her father Mr. Thomas.

When their conversation was done, a delighter Mrs. Thomas came forward, "Congratulations Vidya!" she said, sounding elated.

Vidya walked out of the room coldly without responding. Ann was furious. She did not approve of the way Vidya treated her mother. She walked up the stairs and knocked hard on Vidya's door.

"Vidya, that was very rude. How could you do that?"

"Do what?" Vidya tried to feign ignorance.

"How ungrateful can you be? Your mother worked hard with you over the weekend and you do not have the courtesy even to acknowledge it?"

"What do you want me to do?"

"Why Vidya? Why? Why do you do this to her?"

"Alright Ann, not again. Don't spoil my moment. If you want me to thank her, I will, but don't start again, please."

Vidya walked out of the room and straight to Mrs. Thomas.

"Thank you!"

It was a very dry thank you. Nonetheless, Mrs. Thomas smiled warmly in return, even if her pain was evident.

CHAPTER 32

Love Finds Its Way

When Vidya was 13, Craig, a tall, smart, charming boy, moved into the neighbourhood and joined the same school. He was soon part of Vidya's group of friends— Eric and his sister Paula, Helena and Sherry, who were in the same grade as Vidya, and Joe, who was a year older than Vidya. Craig was in Joe's class. Life became more interesting with Craig hanging out with them.

Craig was an athlete. He loved sports and they would all go cycling in the neighbourhood. They played football, but their favourite pastime was venturing out into the woods. Craig would often climb trees and Vidya thought of him as the Tarzan of the group. She imagined herself to be Jane. She loved the idea. She hugged the idea to herself and was wrapped up in it. She loved being with Craig so much so that she would lose all track of time. Vidya did not realise it, but it was her first crush. She started blushing when anybody talked about him, and paying extra attention to how she looked and dressed, something that hadn't interested her much till then.

"We're going camping in the woods tomorrow, and I want to bake the best cookies".

Ann and Mrs. Thomas were surprised. Vidya . . . No, it was Jane now. Vidya had never shown interest in baking before.

"Of course, dear," said a delighted Mrs. Thomas. "I'll bake you some fresh ones and pack you some sandwiches".

"You did not listen to what I said," she paused for a moment, "I said *I* want to bake cookies."

She always spoke defiantly and rudely when she was with her mother and it hurt Mrs. Thomas. Ann had succeeded in being a friend, a confidante, but the more Mrs. Thomas wanted to sort things out, the worse it got. She was at a loss. She wanted to hug Vidya and pamper her. Mr. Thomas tried to back up his wife, as did Ann, but it was all in vain.

Vidya knew well that there was nobody better than Mrs. Thomas at baking and she wanted to impress her friends, Craig in particular. Softening her tone, she asked, "Will you please teach me how to bake?"

Mrs. Thomas was more than happy. She would do anything for Vidya. She believed that Jesus would one day bridge the gap between them. She was a strong believer and went to church every Sunday to pray to Jesus. She believed that Jesus would answer her prayers.

The camp was a great success. Vidya's friends could not stop raving about the cookies and sandwiches, and she boasted that she had made them herself. Craig had an extra helping which made Vidya even happier.

Now, quite some time was spent in the kitchen on weekends when she wanted to cook something or the other and take it with her. She knew well that Craig was a big foodie and. Sometimes, she called her friends over for tea. Her Tarzan was always a part of it.

"Honey, what's going on?" Ann asked her one evening.

"What's going on?" Vidya was puzzled.

"Nothing in particular, was just wondering."

"Wondering what?"

"Aren't you taking too long in front of that mirror?"

Vidya was taken by surprise. She felt as though her secret was out. Her heart skipped a beat.

Ann gave her a sly smile and she blushed.

"So?"

"So what?"

"Come on Vidya, you know what I am talking about. Maybe I can help you."

Vidya rushed to close the door.

"Ann, please. How?"

A little bit of coaxing and she confided in Ann, but with a promise.

"Does Craig like you too?"

"Oh no! He doesn't know about it."

"Why not?"

Vidya was silent. Ann enjoyed the moment as smiled.

"I don't know if he loves me."

"You need to find out."

"How?"

And they spoke for hours as Ann guided her. Ann did not want Vidya to be hurt. She knew how important a crush seemed at her tender age. Vidya was growing up physically, mentally and emotionally.

CHAPTER 33

Not Easy To Say Goodbye

Fate had never been fair very to Vidya. It did not intend to change. Craig hadn't even been there for a year, and his father was transferred to Beijing on a promotion. The whole family had to leave. Vidya was heartbroken. She had not even confessed her love to Craig. He was her first crush. She was left alone, while her Tarzan packed bags, unaware of the fact that someone loved him so much. So much that it hurt!

"Darling, just go tell him that you like him." Ann was worried about Vidya.

Vidya was inconsolable. "Ann, it's my fate. It will not let anyone whom I love be with me." She sobbed. "Let him go, let him go unhurt."

"Shhh . . . Don't talk like that. It's not right. And why blame yourself?"

"What's going on here?" It was Mr. Thomas who entered the room.

There was silence. Vidya tried to hide her tears and turned away to wipe them, but it was a little too late.

"Ann, I speak to you, will anyone tell me what happened? Why is Vidya crying?"

Ann looked at Vidya and then at Mr. Thomas.

"Oh, nothing much. It's Craig, her best friend, he is leaving tomorrow with his family to China and Vidya is upset about losing a dear friend."

"Oh! Come here, honey!" Mr. Thomas stretched his big arms to embrace Vidya. "You worry a lot. There is always a way to keep in touch. I'm sure you can write to each other. I know it hurts but then, you should be more understanding. And then, there is the telephone."

"No. I don't understand." Vidya was a bundle of roiling emotions and about to explode.

"I don't understand why people I like or love need to go out of my life. I don't understand why God has picked me to be hurt, always. I don't understand why Nana, and Sai," she broke down.

It had been years. Vidya had been happy, adapted well to the changes, but there always was something she held in her heart. Something she never discussed. The Thomases, Ann, and her teachers had never talked about her past. They thought that since she'd been so young then, she barely remembered any of it. It was now obvious that Vidya had been living in her own bubble.

That night, the truth was brought to light. The bubble burst as Vidya bared her soul. Vidya had not forgotten. The wound was still festering, hidden carefully until then. The love for her Nana, Thaatha and little Sai, and the betrayal of her mother. She sobbed her heart out for the first time, talking about her birth family as went back to her past with its simple carefree life, the fields, the cows, the old squeaky cycle, her small hut, the train. And then came the floods; she narrated how she'd lost her family one by one and how her mother left little Sai with her never to come back. She had run away with her lover. How Sai's little body had burnt against her chest and how the Municipality had taken Sai away, and how she'd been brought to the orphanage and then sold to the Thomases.

"So you see, I don't understand a lot of things."

It was a long night. There was shock and silence. Every word Vidya uttered seemed to stab them. Unbelievable! And all the while, Mr. and Mrs. Thomas had believed the story Kamala had fed them, that Vidya was an orphan. Her mother had died during childbirth and her father in an epidemic soon after. Pieces of the puzzle started fitting together. Mr. Thomas now understood why although they showered her with so much love, Vidya was still detached. Why it was difficult for her to accept Mrs. Thomas as her mother. They were aghast.

It was past midnight when Vidya fell asleep, her sobs finally subsiding.

As reality started sinking in, so did the agony of a young girl and her suffering. Mr. Thomas sat, thinking about that day years ago. Agreed, they hadn't had much time, had taken an instant liking for Vidya, but had he let his emotions get the better of his wisdom? He was angry, with himself, the people at the orphanage from where he had adopted Vidya. They'd played their cards well. Got the paperwork filed before the ink was dry. There had been no hint of anything amiss. He should have done a background check. If only he had known the truth. They would still have welcomed Vidya into their family as happily as they had, but they would've known, been better prepared, handled situations differently. Vidya had suffered then and was suffering now. Would her wounds ever heal? Was it too late? It was a rude awakening. Something had to be done.

It was also a difficult time for Mrs. Thomas. She was depressed. Ann and Mr. Thomas tried to preserve a sense of normalcy in the house.

Mr. Thomas had sleepless nights, spoke to his friend who suggested counselling. But would Vidya agree? And there was Social Services to fear. The couple did not wish to lose Vidya.

It wasn't just Vidya. Mrs. Thomas too needed help. It was not going to be easy. Mr. Wilson, his close friend, advised him to report the case to the authorities. Logically it was the right thing to do, but it wasn't easy. When the person in question is close to your heart, your own, you tend to think with the heart, not the head. Practicality takes a backseat. Again, how could he put Vidya through even more! Life had not been fair to her; he could not make it worse. What if she was taken away from them? He was not ready for it, nor would Mrs. Thomas ever be. He had to think of alternatives.

Mr. Thomas was used to stress. He never buckled under pressure, but now he felt helpless. There were so many questions and no answers. Smoke filled the study as sat on the armchair, lost in thought, looking at the sky as though seeking an answer.

CHAPTER 34

Margaret

It was Ann who introduced Margaret to Vidya. Mrs. Thomas knew Margaret well.

"Vidya, I want you to meet my cousin, Margaret."

"Hi Vidya! So you are the wonderful little angel Ann keeps telling me about." Margaret extended her hand.

"Hi," Vidya smiled back.

"Margaret is going to take my place here for a while, until I come back from my honeymoon."

Ann was getting married to Mark, an up-and-coming artist she had met last year at a showing.

"Oh!"

"I'm sure you'll like her too! She's lot more fun."

Vidya was going to miss Ann, but it was her wedding. She was so excited about it. Vidya had been helping Ann with the shopping. Mark and Ann made a good couple. Mark was a great painter. He had shown Vidya his paintings and she loved them. He had promised to do her portrait after they returned from their honeymoon. With Mrs. Thomas not very well, there had to be someone around; someone as reliable as Ann. Margaret had come to fill in.

"Don't you worry, we're going to have some great times. I hear you like riding?"

Vidya was instantly interested in Margaret. She soon found out that Margaret and she shared a passion for adventure.

Margaret's stay at the Thomases' was short, but fruitful. She had brought back Vidya's smile. Very tactfully, she had got Vidya to focus on the brighter side of life. They would spend hours in the garden looking at stars, discussing their interests. They went out fishing, shopping, spent time in the kitchen. Margaret had been to Africa and China, and taught Vidya a few simple dishes. Vidya was a fast learner and enjoyed cooking. It was therapeutic.

Time flew and Vidya grew up to be a confident young lady. Mr. Thomas hoped Vidya would be interested in getting a management degree at college; after all she was the one who would hold the reins of his company one day. But Vidya was happier globe-trotting with her camera. She had taken up journalism. The family was very proud of her.

CHAPTER 35

Bill

It was in Afghanistan that she met Bill. Vidya was working as a freelancer for a big publishing house. There was a lot of political unrest and a lot to cover. Vidya loved to be right in the thick of it all. She loved to capture history as it was being made. It worried her parents, but they knew her she was happy.

"Take good care of yourself, stay safe," the Thomases would tell her when they called her every single day.

"Oh, sure! Don't you worry."

The conversations were short, but it kept them close.

Bill was a well-known face in the media world, and they met one evening at a dinner hosted after a conference. Bill was tall and very handsome with hypnotic eyes. His smile captivated Vidya when he spoke.

"Hi, Vidya," Bill called out, walking towards her.

"Hi," Vidya was happy to meet him.

"I'm a great fan of your work, lady! Love what you do."

"Like what?"

"I mean the stories that you cover, your pictures, they're so surreal. It's like they speak for themselves, touch the heart! I mean, wow!"

"Thanks! I didn't know I had a following!" she smiled. "I've seen some of your work as well. It's not too shabby," she joked. "No, really, I quite admire your style, too."

Vidya covered subjects that made sure that the world didn't ignore pain and suffering in war-torn regions. She had won awards for her work, becoming quite successful. She worked hard; she related to the subject so much that it showed in her work.

The evening was good, the dinner better and the company the best part about it. She liked Bill. They talked, and Vidya found him to be quite intelligent, which was more attractive to her than his handsome face.

He asked for a dance and she obliged.

Later, when it was time to go back, Bill asked, "So, what do you think?"

"Well! Let's see!"

"What's there to see? We can team up and it would be interesting."

"I know, but . . ."

"Come on, what's with your adventurous streak?"

"I hardly know you!"

"Well, in that case lady, let me introduce myself again. Hi Vidya, I'm Bill Morgan. I am . . ."

"Stop that, I know you!"

"Now, make up your mind, do you know me or don't you?" Bill looked her in her eyes. There was an amused, teasing light in his.

"Good night." Vidya turned and walked off.

"See ya tomorrow!"

"We'll see."

"Good! At eight for breakfast, then!" Bill called out.

Vidya shook her head as she walked towards her hotel suite.

Bill had obviously been flirting and surprisingly, she'd enjoyed the attention. She liked Bill's flamboyance.

She thought of him as she took a shower. She could still feel his warm breath from when they had danced together.

"We'll see!" she said, this time to herself, putting on her delicate satin and lace short night dress; her hair still wet as it spread over the pillow like dark mist.

Vidya didn't sleep very well that night. She seemed to have noticed every hour from when she went to bed till dawn. She lay on the soft white linen, looking out of the window. She had yet to write her story and prepare the presentation, but all she could think of was Bill. The sky was clear and the stars bright. Vidya took a deep breath as she finally fell asleep at the break of dawn, still thinking of Bill.

Trrrrrrnnnnnnnnggggggggg . . . Vidya stretched out her arm, reaching for the phone.

"Hello!" her eyes were still closed and voice sleepy.

"Hey! Don't tell me you are still in bed! I've been waiting for you for over half an hour!"

Vidya woke up with a start. "Bill!"

"Yeah! Who else did you promise breakfast?"

"Breakfast? I did not promise anything!"

"Oh yes you did!"

"No I didn't!"

"Alright, now that I have been waiting for you, why don't you just come and join me?"

"Oh, okay. Give me ten minutes. I'll be down"

"Sure, ten minutes it is then."

As Vidya stepped out of bed, she wondered why she had said yes. But wasn't that what she wanted?

It was past nine when as Vidya walked into the lobby, looking lovely in a beautiful cotton floral sleeveless dress with a scoop neckline. The removable skinny belt at the waist showed off her slim waist. She had let her hair loose, and she knew she looked gorgeous.

"Aah! What's on your mind?" asked Bill with a wink.

"Nothing! Should I be thinking of something?"

"Be honest, haven't you been thinking of me?"

"Of course not! Why would I?" Vidya did not look Bill in the eye as she tried to hide her blush.

"You look beautiful when you lie!"

"Come on! Stop flirting. I'm starved!"

It was a beautiful morning. They had scrambled eggs with bacon and baked beans. Vidya found it hard to keep her eyes away from Bill even as she relished the butter and herb button mushrooms with grilled tomatoes.

Bill was wearing a white cotton shirt and khaki shorts, perfect for a summer day. He was definitely handsome, and there was a certain charm about him which must've floored the ladies.

As Vidya took a sip of decaffeinated coffee Bill asked, "So, partner, what do you suggest?"

"Suggest what?"

"Now that we're a team, we need a plan."

"Team? Plan? What're you talking about? I never agreed to anything."

"But you still came for breakfast, didn't you?"

"That is different."

"And I'm sure you will agree to this as well!"

"That confident, are you?"

"That's the way I am and I have never been wrong."

"Then be sure the shock of the first time doesn't floor you!"

"Well, we'll see. Is it a challenge?"

"I don't know anything about your project."

"Great! Then finish your coffee and I'll show you the details."

"It's Sunday, and I am not done with my story yet."

"You can do that later in evening I'm sure."

Curiosity got the better of her then. "Alright then, but just to talk about it." Vidya grabbed her hat as she got up.

Bill was a ladies' man, but when it came to business, he was a thorough professional and better organised than Vidya expected. He spoke at length about the project. Vidya loved the idea of travelling across Africa covering the entire landscape. They would also help raise funds for a couple of NGOs that worked in certain areas. It was the offer of a lifetime. She could feel her enthusiasm rising and Bill's passion was contagious. She felt as though the project was meant for her.

"Well, it's a good proposition, but why me rather than all those brilliant journalists out there?" Vidya couldn't help asking.

"I've seen your work. I love the way you do things, and apart from that I wanted someone beautiful with a wild streak. You're perfect for the job."

"So you came all the way from London to offer me a project?"

"Not really, I'm here for work. But when I saw you, I thought, why not?"

"Hmm, I like the idea, but let me think about it." Vidya had picked up a few traits from Mr. Thomas. She was frank and believed in taking decisions after consideration.

"Alright, take your time. Until tomorrow then."

"Yeah sure, see you tomorrow."

It was almost noon by the time Vidya bid Bill goodbye. She had loads of work to be do. She rushed back to her suite, sketching out a strict schedule for herself.

It was not long before Vidya signed the contract. She'd always worked on her own terms. Bill was more than happy to accommodate a few.

CHAPTER 36

Ranger National Park

Mr. Thomas was happy for Vidya and Mrs. Thomas worried as usual. Vidya and Bill worked out all the details. About five months, many afternoons over cups of coffee and heated discussions later, they finally had their crew in place and ready. It would be almost a year before they came back. Mrs. Thomas's eyes filled as she said goodbye and hugged Mr. Thomas tight. Their mission would study ecology, local habitat and customs, and they would report on problems in the region, including with education and depletion of resources. It was an ambitious and adventurous project with a lot of travelling, research and hardship.

As Vidya spent time more with Bill, she was drawn to him. His passion for his work, the depth of his knowledge and his entertaining stories made him an ideal companion as well as colleague.

The drive to Ranger National Park was pleasant. The weather was warm and just right. They were to camp at the Peacock Bridge, in the very lap of nature. The cottages were simple and clean, with thatched roofs. As Vidya opened the curtains of her room she stopped a moment and took in the view. Unsullied nature – it'd become such a rarity.

"Ah! What a lovely day!"

The day had just begun and the team was excited. They all settled down just in time for a Safari trip organised by the camp. Vidya was pepped up. Grabbing her hat and sunglasses, she rushed out to be greeted by Akiiki, their guide for the tour. Akiiki was young and looked as strong as a bull. He had been working as a guide for a while and knew the terrain well. He was one of the few who spoke English quite well. He was jovial and quite popular as a guide.

"Karibu," He said in Swahili, then switched to English. "Welcome. I am Akiiki, your guide."

"Oh hello Akiiki! Nice to meet you. I am Bill and this is Vidya."

"Hello, Ma'am!"

"Hello! I am looking forward to an exciting day!" Vidya was thrilled. She loved travelling and adventure as much as she loved meeting new people and making friends.

"Yes, of course!"

After a brief session about the dos and don'ts in the jungle, they set off. Bill and Vidya sat in the front, not wanting to miss anything. The road was clear, with green grass and trees on both sides. It was so peaceful and relaxing. They could hear the sounds of the jungle— the chirping of the birds, calls of the animals and the wind. It'd got quite hot, and they were grateful for their broad-brimmed hats and bottles of water. As they drove, their Jeep squeaked and rattled. It was a bumpy ride on the trail. They strained their eyes to catch a glimpse of the animals.

"It is all luck," Akiiki told them. "There are lucky days when you spot the wild animals, and some days, you may not see much. But either way, the jungle is always exciting."

As they moved on Akiiki pointed towards a tree, all heads turned. "See there, on that tree, it is the African Barred Owlet."

Only experienced guides like Akiiki could've spotted such birds perched on the tree. They always know where to find what in the jungle. The tourists simply miss such things.

"Ah! It's so beautiful," said Vidya, adjusting her camera lens to capture the bird. Perched on the branch was a round-headed bird with bright yellow eyes.

As they moved ahead they got to see the Tsessebe back riding an African buffalo.

Akiiki proved to be an excellent guide. He told stories of the jungle when he had witnessed lions attacking elephants. He spoke of the hippos and their fights. Vidya wished she could witness some of it firsthand.

As though answering her prayers, she heard a trumpet as the driver slowed down.

"All silent, don't make noise or move much," Akiiki instructed the team.

Vidya was ready with her camera as a herd of huge elephants crossed the mud track. All of them gasped on seeing the majestic animals with their big tusks—some of them must have been at least two metres—and their muscular trunks. They flapped their big ears. Vidya clicked happily as Bill captured the moment on video.

They declared it had been an excellent day as they returned to the camp and had chilled beer. The evenings were alive with camp fire and there was tribal dance performance for the tourists. Vidya sat close to Bill.

"How long are you going to stay here?" Akiiki asked. "I hear you have booked the cottage for a long time."

"Yes. We may stay here for a few months. We have come to see and understand your country, culture and more," said Bill as Vidya digged into the Sosatie. It was spicy and yummy.

"Oh, I see. You can call me anytime you need help," Akiiki offered.

"Sure will,"

Akiiki proved to be very helpful as he arranged for Vidya and Bill to meet the forest rangers and officials. There were a lot of permissions and approvals to be taken before they could venture deep into the forest where they could witness the real wild.

Work progressed satisfactorily and Vidya and Bill grew closer. They could no longer ignore their attraction and the beauty of the jungle kindled that flame.

The sun was setting and the view was panoramic as Vidya walked outside. Bill was standing near the edge of the garden lost in thoughts.

"Hey there!" Vidya's greeting brought Bill back from his thoughts as he looked at her.

"Hi! Come on."

The bonfire was being set alight. It would be dark soon, but there was still time for dinner. She was done with her work for the day and had had a shower. She looked fresh and beautiful. Bill could hardly take his eyes off her.

As the day faded, Vidya's beauty glowed in the radiance of the bonfire. The beautiful music stirred other fires.

"You light my nights and my dreams
I love you so you know . . . ."

Their eyes met as Bill reached for Vidya's hand. Vidya did not resist. They did not speak.

"Roses and thorns may come along
But my love will grow you know . . ."

Bill leaned forward as Vidya closed her eyes and raised her face. As their lips met, the song in the background seemed to be sung to the rhythm of their hearts. Time itself seemed to stop as they were lost in each other. She drew closer, running her fingers gently through Bill's hair; she could feel his breath as he held her in his strong arms as if she were the most precious thing in his life.

"We are one, come rain or sun,
Like the rainbow . . . .
I love you so you know . . . ."

CHAPTER 37

Bleeding Wounds

It was late in the afternoon; they had been in the jungle the whole morning trying to capture the action of the wild. They had been filming for hours when suddenly the monkeys started screeching. Vidya raised her camera as she saw movement in the bush. There was a strong and imposing buffalo with her calf. As Vidya focused her camera, she could see the wounds on the buffalo's back. The calf was sticking beside her and she looked anxious. Suddenly she saw three lions surround them and then with lightening speed, they attacked the calf. The mother buffalo bellowed and started attacking the lions. It was a brave fight to save her young one. The camera rolled, capturing the action. The buffalo fought until the lions conceded defeat, but not before injuring her further. Blood trickled from the wounds as she stood guard.

Vidya knew it would not be long before the mother succumbed and the calf would be all alone to fend for himself. She felt Bill's fingers wipe her tears.

"Hush! It's fine. Come here!" He held her in his arms, close to his chest as Vidya sobbed. She was sad throughout the evening. Bill tried to cheer her up but in vain.

"I thought you were strong." He said. "If you do not like it, you need not come for the shoots." There was concern in his voice.

"Bill you do not understand . . ." Vidya's voice broke as she spoke.

"It's fine. You can cover your feature with the tribes and I will get help from the crew. Don't you worry, darling!'

Vidya was quiet for some time; she looked aimlessly at the sky and broke down again.

"Dear, what happened?" Bill was worried.

"I just hope the mother buffalo lives," her voice trailed off. "Not everyone is as fortunate as the little calf in the jungle whose mother protected him so fiercely," she went on after a moment.

"Why do you say so?"

It would be another long night. Vidya had never thought she would ever speak about all those things again. But the incident had shaken her. She told Bill all about herself, how she had lost her family and how Amma had disowned her and Sai.

Bill held her tight as she cried.

"No one is as unfortunate as I am."

"That's not true!"

"Oh Bill, you will never understand," she sobbed.

CHAPTER 38

A Realisation

Mr. Thomas kept in touch with Vidya. She spoke to him at length, sharing her experiences. She was happy, but her conversations with Mrs. Thomas remained a formality. She knew that it would please her father, so she spoke to Mrs. Thomas polite, civil, short conversations as if between strangers. Bill had noticed the behaviour earlier, but now he understood the reason why.

"Come quick, love, we are already late," Bill called to Vidya as she came out of the cottage.

"Sorry, was up late last night."

Akiiki was waiting in the car as Bill and Vidya got in.

"How long will it take?"

"We will be there before noon," Akiiki responded as the driver revved the engine and they drove towards the village.

"We need to stop by some shops and bakery to buy stuff for the children," Vidya reminded Akiiki.

"Yes, I remember. We will have time if you don't take long."

Bill and Vidya picked up some toys and candies for the children in the orphanage. As they reached the gates, they saw kids playing in the open. They seemed to be a happy bunch chasing and running around, laughing loudly. They stopped when they saw the visitors. A lady came forward to greet them and Akiiki was the translator.

It was almost Christmas and so Vidya felt it would be the right time for gifts — her way of contributing, which she always did, wherever she went. She always raised funds and donated what she could. It made her happy. She loved the smiles on the faces of little angels as she distributed the candies. She hugged them, ruffled their hair and smiled gently. They spent the whole day interacting with the kids, trying to get to know them. Vidya played games with them. There was a smile of sheer happiness on Vidya's face as they bid goodbye in the evening.

"Bill, I am going to adopt a child," Vidya told Bill on their way back.

"I don't think you should."

Vidya was taken aback. "What?"

"I said I don't think you should."

"Why not? They are such angels, they are divine, and how can you say so?"

"Who knows what they are?"

"You are being rude." There was anger in Vidya's voice.

"I am being frank and honest."

"What do you mean?"

"I mean, how can you judge them? They do look like angels, but they can spell trouble and make your life hell. I don't think they can be trusted. They can't be loved selflessly. I think it's a bad idea."

"They can't be trusted? Why not?" Vidya's voice was raised. "All that they want is love, a sense of belonging, and they deserve as much of a chance in life as the other privileged kids. A chance to grow, a chance to live."

"Well, I reserve my opinion."

"Then you are wrong **Mr. Morgan,**" she exclaimed, hurt and anger in her voice. Akiiki tried not to listen to their conversation and did not interrupt.

"I told you earlier, I am never wrong, **Ms. Thomas,** never wrong. These kids are not worth the effort. They will never understand **selfless** love and the sacrifice and pain a parent would go through to bring smiles on their face. They are all self-centred; they love being pitied; they're happy being underprivileged. They never grow up, they love to live in their past. They cannot understand love."

"Stop the car!" Vidya almost shouted.

The car screeched to a halt as Vidya got down and slammed the door.

"I thought you were a good man Mr. Morgan, but it seems now that I was wrong." Her voice shook. "I was wrong. I don't think we can work or stay together anymore."

Then she turned to Akiiki. "Can you arrange another car for me? I am not going to travel with him."

Akiiki looked at Bill and then got out of the car.

"I was wrong, so wrong," Vidya repeated.

"Yes, you were wrong, very wrong. Wrong all along. Look into yourself, Vidya, and you will understand what I say."

"Keep your opinion to yourself Mr. Morgan. If you have a heart, it's made of stone."

There was a bus coming along and Vidya waved her hand. The bus driver seemed confused as the bus slowed down and when he saw Vidya walking towards the bus that the driver stepped on the brakes. Vidya got on the bus along with Akiiki.

Back in the cottage, Vidya cried out loud. "How could Bill be so nasty?" She'd thought he loved her. He knew about her, about her past. She had shared everything with him and this was the last thing she had expected from a person she always thought was sensible and caring.

"I am not going to stay here any longer," she said to herself as she packed her bags.

She had asked Akiiki to book her tickets.

"The first flight out of here," she emphasised.

The earliest flight Akiiki could manage was in two days later. Vidya did not join Bill for lunch. She did not go out for tea, either.

Her heart was heavy and she felt lonely and let down. Tears flowed as she dialled the number. She wanted to speak to Mr. Thomas. He had always been so understanding. She needed him so much now. It was Mrs. Thomas who answered the phone.

"Hi, it's Vidya."

"Oh hello darling! What a wonderful surprise. How good to hear from you!" Mrs. Thomas sounded so pleased to speak to Vidya.

"Yes, how are you?" Vidya asked flatly.

"What happened, dear? Is everything fine?"

"Yes, it's all fine."

"You don't sound like it. Vidya, please tell me, is there something you want?"

Vidya got irritated. Why did Mrs. Thomas have to be so annoying?

"Can I please speak to Dad," she cut Mrs. Thomas short.

"Sure, honey." Mrs. Thomas sounded dejected as she handed the phone over to Mr. Thomas. She knew well that Vidya tended to be petulant when pushed and did not probe further.

Vidya was too upset. She needed so badly to speak to her father, but Mrs. Thomas had irritated her so much that she did not talk as much as she would have liked to. Mr. Thomas was understanding as always. His warmth came through his words. He assured her of his love and support.

"Do you want us to come there for some time, darling?" he asked.

"No, I'm fine. I'll take care of myself." Vidya cut the conversation short. She had put the phone on the speaker as she sat on the bed packing her bags.

"So you see, I was not wrong. I never am!" Vidya was startled as she turned around to see Bill in her room, leaning against the wall. She'd been so engrossed that she had not noticed Bill come in.

"How dare you? And what do you mean by 'You are never wrong'?"

"I asked you to look into yourself, but looks like you did not."

"Why and what should I be introspecting Mr. Counsellor?"

"Look into yourself, Vidya, your relationship with your mother, and be fair in your judgement. I will be waiting for you for dinner tonight." Bill walked out before Vidya could respond.

Vidya swore as she sat on the bed, her eyes on the empty wall. It was as though someone had slapped her hard, as though she'd been stabbed in the heart. She sat there like a log, feeling as if her heart was weighing her down. She cried. She wailed. Bill heard her cry; he stopped and turned, before walking away resolutely.

Dinner was served, but Bill's plate was empty. He sat on the chair staring at the bonfire, sipping his whiskey. This was his fourth drink but he did not enjoy the drink. He felt a hand on his shoulder and turned around to see Vidya standing behind him. Her eyes were red and swollen; she looked sad, had not changed nor showered.

"Bill . . . ."

Bill got up. Vidya hugged him and broke down.

"You were right," she said between sobs. "I was wrong, so wrong." She could only whisper, barely getting the words out as shuddering sobs wracked her body.

Bill cradled her face in his palms and looked into her eyes. "It's not late. It never is."

"Oh Bill, but how?"

"Mothers need no reason. Trust me, they do not need any. It's time you gave her what she truly deserves. It's time to undo the wrong. It's Christmas. Go, go give her the gift of love."

"But how?"

"Just a hug . . . . that's all it takes."

Vidya nodded. Bill wiped her tears and then planted a kiss on her beautiful lips. They had dinner together after all.

CHAPTER 39

The Perfect Proposal

Since the flight was in two days, Akiiki had arranged for them to visit the tribal colony. The crew was as excited as Vidya. They had worked hard for this opportunity and today was even more special. After a long drive in the Jeep, they had to walk into the interiors of the jungle for many miles before they came to the village.

Vidya was fascinated. It all seemed so festive and vibrant. The tribesmen wore headgear with colourful feathers and the women wore beautiful beads in their hair, around their waists and arms, their bodies painted with chalk. They were performing their ritual dance. Bill and Vidya joined them following their steps carefully, wide smiles lighting up their faces.

Vidya was surprised young men looking worried but determined as the celebrations progressed. Akiiki explained that the young men had to prove that they were no longer boys, but strong and brave young men by jumping over the bulls. The successful were declared adults and eligible to marry, while the others had to wait for another year to prove themselves. The women looked lovely in their goat-skin skirts.

Vidya held her breath as she watched the men jumping over the bulls. A few were successful and were cheered, while many fell and hurt themselves.

The men then battled it out with a stick called *donga*. The winner was given chance to choose his bride.

"Oh! I never thought the tribesmen would be so romantic, that they would fight to win their brides," Vidya said.

"Hmm. Love is not easy, not in the jungle, not the city."

"Oh, yeah! Do you think the educated and the sophisticated would ever dare such dangerous games to win a girl?"

"Yeah, I think you have a point there."

As Vidya was engrossed in the festivities, Bill talked to Akiiki, who explained more. A girl came forward and tugged at Vidya's hand, encouraging her to join the dance. They gave her headgear of beautiful feathers which she wore and posed happily for pictures. She danced with the girls, joining hands in a circle as the elderly women cheered and sang aloud. She turned to see that Bill also wearing a headgear and joining the men for a drink. Their eyes met and she smiled as they danced.

Suddenly there were loud cheers. Vidya and the other women turned to see the bulls lining up. They all moved towards the crowd. The drums beat louder as the men clapped.

Vidya was shocked. "No" she cried. "No, Bill, no!"

Bill was standing with a large wooden jug in his hand. He took a large sip, looked at Vidya and sprinted. He'd been an athlete in college, but that was then. He was agile and strong still, but this was a different game altogether. The cheering grew louder as Vidya held her breath. Bill jumped over the bulls, clearing them at one go and stood up, both his hands up in the air in victory. Vidya could not believe her eyes. She stood there, dumbstruck. Bill then went ahead and lifted a donga and asked Akiiki to join him. Vidya started enjoying the game now. She joined the group to cheer Bill. The stick fight was symbolic and Bill was declared the winner.

As Bill walked towards Vidya, she blushed. Bill plucked a flower from bush, got down on one knee and proposed to Vidya.

"Yes!" Vidya shouted and hugged him. Bill kissed her as if he'd never let her go.

There was an even louder cheer, more dancing, drinking and fun. It was a day Vidya would never forget.

Their stay in Africa was hugely successful, professionally and personally. Bill joined Vidya on her flight back home.

Chapter 40

A Sense Of Belonging

As they stepped out of the airport, Bill assured Vidya that everything would be fine. Vidya was nervous. Bill had wanted Vidya to call her parents and inform them of her arrival, but Vidya wanted it otherwise. She knew that her parents would have gone to the church as usual on Sunday and would not be home when she reached.

She stopped to buy bright purple orchids on her way. Mrs. Thomas loved orchids. She also bought a card. As the taxi stopped at the cul-de-sac, Vidya felt as nervous as she had felt the first time she stepped into the house years ago. She had her set of keys. She paid the taxi and entered. This time, she felt a sense of belonging. It was *her* house, her very own. She went into her room, unpacked and had a shower. There was still some time for Mr. and Mrs. Thomas to return.

She picked up the orchids and went into her parents' room, placed the orchids in the vase and kept it beside the bed. She quickly penned a few words—*"Love you Mom! Vidya"*—on the card and placed it beside the vase before walking out of the room. They were simple words, but she had written them from the very depths of her heart. There were tears in her eyes, but these tears did not hurt her. They gave her a sense of relief. But she was still nervous. She then went into the kitchen and cooked a meal for her family.

The table was laid just in time — she heard the car pulling into the drive just as she finished. Feeling nervous but mischievous, she hid — it would be a real surprise.

As the door opened she saw her parents enter. **Mr. and Mrs. Thomas, her Dad and Mom.** They made such a good couple, but they looked tired and old. She wanted to run and hug them, but held herself back.

Vidya tiptoed after her parents as they entered their bedroom. They were indeed surprised to find the fresh and beautiful orchids.

"Oh, darling! Thank you so much, they are beautiful!" Mrs. Thomas said, bending to smell the flowers.

"But dear! They're not from me!" Mr. Thomas was equally surprised.

"Come on! Who else could it be? I know how much you love me." Mrs. Thomas sat on the bed, picked up the card and opened to read it aloud.

"Love you Mom! Vidya"

The couple looked at each other as Vidya stepped into the room. All eyes were moist. Mrs. Thomas opened her arms as Vidya rushed to hug her. She cried, as did her Mom.

Bill was right, mothers do not need a reason or words for love. They had lunch together. Their family was complete in the truest sense this Christmas. Jesus had finally answered Mrs. Thomas's prayers. In the evening, they all went to the church to light candles. They talked about everything, and Vidya gushed on and on about Bill. Her Mom smiled to see her as much in love as she'd always been with her husband.

They were happy for Vidya and Bill.

Bill introduced Vidya to his parents, who declared that they loved her already.

Now Vidya spent more of her time with Mrs. Thomas, sharing her thoughts and much more. They went out shopping, to restaurants, salons and more. Mr. Thomas teased them saying that he was being ignored, but it did not matter. He was happy for them and they knew it.

CHAPTER 41

Devi! Have Mercy!

Bill and Vidya continued working together. One evening, after they'd been dating for about six months, time flew as they planned their next project until it was time for dinner.

"Stay for dinner," Bill insisted.

"Alright. But let's make it simple, I'm not too hungry".

"Why don't we go to my place then, we can pick something up on the way."

"Great idea. I'm too tired to dress up."

As they passed the roundabout, the aroma of spices filled the air and was so inviting that they stopped by the *Sizzling Bites* truck parked at the corner, dropping their plans for a lazy dinner. Picking up their food and a six-pack of beer they went to the park.

It had been a while since they had spent a quiet moment together. They settled in a corner behind the thick bush, out of sight of evening joggers and the kids merrily playing on the swings. Vidya rested her head on Bill's shoulder taking a deep breath and losing herself in the moment. The golden rays of the setting sun filtered through the thick canopy of the lush green English oaks. It was a beautiful evening, with a lovely breeze and the grass so soft. Bill leaned to kiss her lips as she closed her eyes, letting herself drown in that tender moment. She could hear the symphony of their breaths as she felt an electric rush through her body. Her heart pounded and she felt light, each muscle relaxing as she surrendered herself into Bill's strong arms.

Vidya bowed her head in front of the Devi; she was clad in a beautiful red silk saree. Bangles tinkled on her wrists and the scent of mogra flowers was so refreshing. She lit the Agarbattis and joined her hands, offering prayers. She prayed for happiness and for a good life with Bill. She turned back to see Bill approaching her with a garland in his hands. She was so happy.

Suddenly, there was chaos. The villagers gathered and started shouting at Vidya. She could not understand what was going on. A strongly-built man came forward and held Bill's hand tight as others surrounded him with sticks and sickles. Vidya was scared. She ran towards Bill.

"Leave him, let him go, leave him," she shouted, but she was held back.

"Vidya, how can you marry someone outside your caste?" they shouted.

"But I love Bill. He loves me. We will be happy."

"You cannot break the rules. The Devi will be angry, very angry and then there will be destruction. We cannot let it happen."

"Kill them! Beat them!" tempers were running high as Bill and Vidya struggled.

Bill managed to break free. He ran towards Vidya and held her hand."Which way?" he asked.

They sprinted towards the exit. They skipped steps and ran across the fields with the villagers following them. Sticks and stones were being pelted at them as they ducked. It had started to drizzle as the clouds became heavy and dark. It started pouring as they raced towards the river. There was a boat on the banks and Vidya got in. Bill pushed it into the rising waters and jumped in before rowing away.

The tide was high and they struggled to keep the boat afloat. They saw the villagers thronging the bank. They were shouting, throwing sticks and sickles. As they rowed away as a big wave washed over the boat, capsizing it. Bill and Vidya were in the cold water as the currents pulled them down.

Vidya struggled to breathe, struggled to swim. She took a big gasp as she frantically searched for Bill in the cold and dark.

"Devi, have mercy!" she cried out.

"Vidya, wake up!" Bill shook her hard as Vidya opened her eyes. She looked around, in confusion and then pure relief as she hugged Bill tight.

"Thank God! Thank you, God!" she was crying.

"What happened honey? It's all fine. It was just a dream!" Bill comforted her.

Vidya nodded. She had long forgotten the story of Krishnudu and Rukumani—or so she'd thought.

CHAPTER 42

No! Not Once Again

Vidya and Bill dated for over two years before they got married. Vidya was a beautiful bride as Mr. Thomas led her proudly to the altar. The night before, she looked at the stars, trying to find her Nana. He would be so happy for her. She wondered how she would look if she wore a silk saree; dressed up as a village bride with mogra flowers. She smiled as she remembered how she would speak to her Nana about her prince charming.

Life was beautiful. Vidya and Bill settled in. Soon, Keith was born. He was a smart kid. As Vidya held Keith for the first time, she could not help but remember Sai, her little brother she loved so much.

Time flew. Almost in a flash, or so it seemed, Keith was six years old.

It was a wonderful morning "I must thank Bill," Vidya said to herself. "If it weren't for him I would never be here." Taking a deep breath and soaking in the freshness of the breeze that gently blew through the valley, she looked around.

It was her land, her country—or was it still? She'd always had a detached attachment to India; the country of her birth and her being. She had many fond memories that brought a happy smile to her face, but then there were the horrors which had ruined a part of her life.

She took another deep breath, trying to put away the depressing thoughts, gazing at the majestic snow-capped mountains of the Himalayas. It was indeed breathtaking. She turned around. Bill was still asleep, his legs stretching across the double bed. Vidya shook her head. "You can never sleep straight," she murmured.

The weather was pleasant and Vidya was ready for their adventure. They had flown down to Delhi, and caught a train to Kalka where they boarded the Toy Train to Shimla, enjoying the lazy yet beautiful journey where they hired a four-wheel drive Jeep. Keith seemed to have taken after his parents. He was enjoying the adventure and was thrilled with the day's itinerary.

"You sure don't want to join us today?" Keith asked his father over breakfast.

"I'd love to darling, but the shoot will get delayed. It's a wonderful day. Enjoy yourself and I will join you by noon."

"I hope you make it by the time we reach the river."

"Sure, love," said Bill, grabbing his leather jacket.

"I'll wait for you, Dad! You know how hysterical Mom is when it comes to water," Keith said, waving as Bill got into the waiting Jeep.

Vidya shuddered, envisioning Keith and Bill in the white waters of the Himalayan river rafting. They had been excited and Vidya had tried to conceal her concerns.

She joined Keith on the gondola. The view was breathtaking from the ropeway. She laughed as Keith stumbled wearing those large skiing shoes. "It's almost noon and we are heading towards the river, where are you, Bill?" Mobile networks were unreliable and Vidya was getting worried.

"I'm on my way, will meet you in an hour," assured Bill over the phone. "Relax darling, enjoy yourself."

"How long will it take?" Keith was thrilled when he spotted the gushing river.

"Fifteen minutes. There seems to be a jam round the corner," replied their driver, Kashinath, carefully manoeuvring through the rugged roads. It was a steep descend and they were driving along the edge of a narrow cliff. A beautiful drive, just the kind of adventure they were looking for. She was uncertain and reluctant at first, but she was glad now that she had come.

The traffic moved at snail's pace and Keith was getting impatient. "Can we walk down? This seems to be taking forever."

"Hold on Keith, we're almost there."

Vidya turned around on hearing loud shouts. "Landslide!" Vidya went numb for a moment. She then grabbed Keith and jumped out of the Jeep just in time as a big boulder tumbled onto the Jeep, veering it off the road and down the cliff, with Kashinath in it. She saw more boulders coming. She now stood on the precarious ledge that was left of the road, with the deep valley yawning at her feet. She wanted to run for cover, but there was nowhere to go. The roads had suddenly disappeared and all that remained were deep gorges as masses of soil and debris slid down uprooting the majestic trees she had admired along the way. Weapons of hell were being hurled at them mercilessly as she desperately looked around for escape. Keith was petrified and held on to Vidya with all his strength. The patch of road on which they stood cracked and Keith slipped along with it.

"Keith!" Vidya shrieked in horror.

"Mom!" Vidya could see her little one falling down, fear on his face, his hand scrabbling for grip, for her hand.

"No! Keith! No!" She jumped after him. It was a bottomless spin as she got covered with silt and stones, rocks bouncing down like deadly missiles seeking to crush them. Bruised and bleeding, she coughed and struggled for breath. Her nails broke and her fingers went numb as she frantically searched for Keith under the rubble.

She used all her strength to move the rocks. She could hear his voice moaning faintly. "I will do it. Yes, I will," she kept repeating, over and over again. She had to dig deep inside her for all the courage she had to save her son. She needed him. She would find him, and save him. She would not lose him.

"You can meet your son now." The doctor's words brought Vidya back to the present.

"How is he, doctor?" Bill asked.

"He will recover, don't you worry."

As Vidya entered the room, she found Keith looking frail and weak, lying on the bed covered with white sheet. His eyes were closed.

"He is under sedation," the nurse told Vidya as she sat on the steel stool beside the bed. She bent down to kiss him gently on the forehead. Bill stood beside her, looking at Keith. There was pain in his eyes, but he kept himself strong.

Mr. and Mrs. Thomas flew down to be with the family. Vidya felt stronger. She told them about the accident and her struggle at Kishen Seth hospital.

"Dad, do you remember the orphanage from where you adopted me?"

Her question surprised everyone.

"Why do you ask?"

"I want to search for Amma—I want to know the truth."

"What truth?" asked Bill.

"You know, when Keith was soaked in blood and lying unconscious on the floor, I did not have money on me and all I wanted at that time was to save Keith. I pleaded and I cried, but there was no one to help. The thought of losing Keith was unbearable. I was ready to do anything at that time. I mean anything, anything at all, to save him. Moral or immoral, right or wrong, none of that mattered."

There was silence in the room as she spoke.

"But I had to leave Keith there alone if I had to get help. It was a difficult decision." She spoke about the paan-chewing, bald attendant. "I did not know if he would really help me, or had the intention of doing so. But I would've done anything he'd asked me to if there'd been just a chance that he'd help me.

Vidya broke down. "Can it not be possible that Amma too had to decide? She was a simple woman from a small village. She was vulnerable, she'd lost everything. She was on the verge of losing her child. How easy would it have been to trick her?"

"It's been a long time, but I know the name of the orphanage. We may get some information there," Mr. Thomas assured Vidya.

It took a week for Keith to get well enough to travel. Bill wanted to stay back with Vidya and help her trace her past, but she insisted that he go along with Keith and Mrs. Thomas.

"Keith will need you!" she said, and there could be no argument.

CHAPTER 43

The Search Begins

So much had changed. Villages had become towns; the cities had state-of-the-art facilities, huge, sleek buildings. Modernisation had touched everything. The country had developed and it showed.

It was difficult to communicate in local language. Gestures and signs did not help much. They decided to hire a special guide as they traced their steps back into the past. It was not an easy task. The city names had changed, as had the street names. Kumar, their guide, was a young man in his early twenties. He tried to help as they got into an autorikshaw searching for Mangalwadi. The auto driver was in his fifties and knew the lanes and by-lanes like the back of his hand.

"*Sahib*! When did you come to the city last?" he asked as Kumar translated the conversation.

"It was years ago," Mr. Thomas replied.

"I thought so. It is not called Mangalwadi any longer. The place has changed, it's New Market now." The auto driver seemed to know a lot.

As they drove through the lanes, Vidya recognised nothing. Gone were the small shops and huts. The place was bustling with activity as people thronged the market place.

"Where do you want to go in New Market?" asked Kumar.

"There was an orphanage. *Innocent Smiles,* that's what it was called."

"I have been to this place several times; I don't think there is any orphanage there." Kumar sounded certain.

"Let us go and check it out."

Vidya felt nervous and uneasy. The journey brought back memories of the past. Horrible memories. She did not know if she could find Amma, and if she found her what would her reaction be? How would Amma respond? What if she found out that Amma had indeed betrayed her? Vidya was silent, but there was a lot going on in her head.

"Can you give me a landmark at least? We cannot go on driving through the lanes like this."

"You were right, the place has changed. I do not recognise anything here." Mr. Thomas sounded discouraged.

"There was a clock tower near the orphanage," Vidya said. She'd suddenly remembered the big clock. She'd been amused to see such a big clock when she was a child.

"Oh! That is on the other part of the street." The auto took a turn and moved in the opposite direction. In less than five minutes, they were in front of the clock tower. It was the same one, Vidya was sure.

Kumar got down and asked the pushcart vendor if he knew where Innocent Smiles was. No one seemed to know the place. It looked like they'd have to give up.

"I think we need to ask someone who has been in this area for a long time. Only they will know." The auto driver went towards a paan shop. The shopkeeper was an old man, busy rolling betel nuts in the green leaves.

"Chacha, how long have you been here?" the auto driver asked the shopkeeper.

"This is an old shop, dear. We have been here for decades. My grandfather set up this paan shop and it is the most famous one here." He seemed to be proud of the quality of paans he sold.

"Yes, I know. Your paans are very famous." Stuffing the beetle leaf into his mouth and chewing it slowly, the auto driver further questioned. "Would you be able to tell us where Innocent Smiles is?"

"Innocent Smiles?"

"Yes, there used to be an orphanage somewhere here."

"Oh, that one, it was shut down years ago. Why do you ask?"

"Nothing, there is someone who wanted to donate to the orphanage. They were here years ago."

"Oh no, no, there is no orphanage here anymore, and moreover, there were raids by the police. The authorities of the orphanage sold kids and they were caught. It was so shocking when we heard it at first." It did not take effort to get out information from the old man.

"Is that so?"

"Yes, we heard that children were stolen and brought here to be sold to the rich and wealthy. That is how they made money. God punishes the wrongdoers. "

"Is there anyone who worked there that you know, any child who stayed in the orphanage—anyone?"

"No. Some were caught and jailed; some escaped. The children were taken by some NGO. No, no one that I know of."

Mr. Thomas could not hide his pain any more. Vidya held his hand. "Dad! You have been the most loving father and I thank God for choosing you for me!"

They returned back to their hotel. It had not been a fruitful day, but neither had it been completely wasted.

"Kumar, I want to go to the temple tomorrow." Vidya said as Kumar was about to leave for the day.

"Sure, Ma'am. I will be here to pick you up after breakfast." He paused."Which temple do you want to visit?"

"The Devi temple"

"Which Devi temple? There is a temple in every nook and corner here. Which one are you talking about?"

Vidya had no answer. She'd been too small then. She remembered a few names, names of people who were close to her or had affected her deeply, but she did not remember the names of places or cities.

"It is a big one; there are steps to climb—around 20 to 30 steps, where old and needy people sit and the devotees offer them alms and food."

"There are many such temples here. Devotees offer alms and food in all such temples." Kumar looked puzzled.

"Let us do one thing, we will go to all such temples tomorrow."

Kumar shrugged his shoulders "Alright, if that is what you want." He was being paid, and paid quite well, so he would do as told.

"Make sure you wash your hair then, you cannot enter the temple without having a proper wash," he said as he closed the door.

Vidya and Kumar went from one temple to another for days. Vidya was sure she would recognise the temple. How could she ever forget the fearful nights she had spent on the temple step, or the tree under which she had tried to shelter Sai, or the shop where Sai was declared dead as she held him tight to her bosom.

Kumar tried to ask her why she was running around town searching for a particular temple when she wasn't even sure which one, but she didn't tell him.. She just asked him to take her to a few more temples. Mr. Thomas accompanied Vidya, but it was too hot and humid outside. He started feeling unwell, and Vidya decided to go with Kumar alone. Mr. Thomas was reluctant, but Vidya was firm.

Bill and Keith spoke to Vidya regularly. Keith missed his mother and Vidya promised that she would be back soon.

"Bill, give me a few more days. Just one more week. I promise to come back then, whether or not I succeed."

Bill understood. "Alright, it's just that Keith is a little uncomfortable and misses you. But don't you worry, I will take care. You just be careful."

"Sure. Thanks, honey."

Time was running out and Vidya could not stay for long. She had a family.

"Kumar, do you know any temple near the bus station?" she asked.

"There are many bus stops and many temples."

"No, not the bus stops, the bus station, from where you go to different towns." Vidya vaguely remembered that she had boarded the bus which took her to the factory and the bus station was close to the temple.

"There are four main bus stations in the city." He answered.

"Good. Take me to all of them and we will try and find the temple."

She prayed at every temple she visited. She hoped that the next day would bring good news. It was like searching for a needle in a haystack.

CHAPTER 44

The Revelation

Vidya wanted to start her day early. This was her last chance. She had not slept well that night and woke up at the crack of dawn. Her legs hurt – she'd walked a lot, climbed up and down so many steps in the last week, in the sweltering heat.

"Vidya, I will accompany you today." Mr. Thomas wanted so much to come along.

"No, Dad! You rest. I will be fine."

"I'm okay now. Besides, there is nothing to do in the hotel suite." He insisted.

"Let him come along. There are only four main bus stations, and we will be able to cover them by noon." Kumar walked in as Vidya and Mr. Thomas sipped coffee.

The first bus station they went to was new; they still went to the temples in the neighbourhood. As the autorikshaw took a turn towards the next bus station, Vidya took a sip of bottled water. They got down and walked towards the temple; Vidya's feet hurried as if of their own volition.

"Madam!" Kumar called out.

"Vidya, wait . . . ." Mr. Thomas was trying to keep up with her.

Vidya turned around. "This is it. This is it!" she cried as people stopped to look at her, but she was oblivious to all that.

It was the same temple. She could recognise it. She ran towards the steps, took off her shoes and raced up. Yes, it was the very same temple. She recognised the deity, the serene smile on her lips and divine face. She folded her hands. She was so excited that she'd forgotten to buy flowers and coconut from one of the shops below. She just stood there with folded hands, brimming with tears.

A pundit was performing puja and she prayed hard. "Devi, help me find my Amma," she pleaded.

Mr. Thomas was panting as he came and stood beside Vidya, a basket of flowers and a coconut in his hand.

With the puja done, Vidya took out some alms and offered them to the old men and women who sat on the temple steps, their palms out. She stopped by every lady trying to recognise if she was her Amma.

Vidya had been so young, about six or seven, and it had been years. She was not sure if she could recognise her mother anymore. She knew her mother's name was Punnu. She asked every woman's name as she offered alms. She was not sure if she would find her mother here, but she hoped she would.

There was no one by the name Punnu and she walked towards the tree where she had taken shelter with Sai on that fateful day. Her heart was heavy and she was quiet; it was as though she had fought with everything she had, but lost the battle.

"Kumar, will you go and ask those people on the temple steps if they know or knew any lady by the name Punnu," Mr. Thomas urged.

Kumar was confused. He stood there, trying to understand.

"Please, Kumar."

Kumar looked embarrassed, but went ahead. He came back after about 20 minutes with no good news.

Vidya stood under the tree looking at the temple without blinking as though expecting a miracle. Mr. Thomas was worried for Vidya.

He stood beside her in her silence.

"Vidya, if I recollect well, you said you took shelter in front of a shop with your brother, would you be able to recognise that shop?"

Vidya turned around. She looked at the row of shops. They were all new structures, but there was one that looked familiar. She walked slowly towards the direction. She stood in front of the shop for some time. She had stood here before, an age ago, so many times, devouring the bright candies in the glass bottles with her eyes. There were orange, yellow, green and red candies. She'd wanted them so much then. Sweet candies, which her mother could not afford. There were no big glass bottles now; they'd been replaced by chocolates in colourful, glossy wraps. She looked at the shutter. It was the very same. She turned and nodded as Mr. Thomas followed her.

There was a young man at the counter. There were a few customers inside and the shopkeeper was busy. Mr. Thomas stepped in and spoke to the young man at the counter.

"Yes sir, what would you like to have?" he asked. He looked educated.

Mr. Thomas asked for a bottle of water and as he paid the bill asked, "Is this your shop?"

"Yes, it is." He answered.

"Hmm." Mr. Thomas was thinking.

"Where have you come from?" asked the man.

"London."

"Oh! Nice place. I have heard of it and seen it in the movies."

Mr. Thomas smiled.

"I need some help from you," Mr. Thomas said. He was not sure if it'd be of any use, but he gave it a try.

"Yes sir, do you want a guide for a city tour? I can arrange one for you."

"No dear, I have a few questions to ask and I think you are the one who can help me find the answers."

"Okay, what do you want to know?"

"What's your name, young man?"

"Ravi."

"Ravi, this shop of yours, has it been your shop for long, or did you buy it recently?"

"This shop was set up by my father. I take care of it now."

"Can I please meet your father?"

"My father? But why?"

"Ravi, please help us. We have come so far, we are searching for someone your father may know."

"Do you know my father?" he asked.

"No, but my daughter may know him." He pointed towards Vidya who was still standing in front of the shop. She had not come in.

"He does not come to the shop now. He is old and weak. If you like, you can come to my house and meet him there."

"Sure, why not. Thank you so much." There was a still hope – not much, but not none.

"Please wait for some time, I need to finish some work and then I will take you."

Mr. Thomas nodded and went out. He spoke to Vidya. She looked hopeful, but unsure.

They walked through the dingy lane, following Ravi, and soon they were in front of a wooden door. He knocked and it opened with a squeak. They saw a veranda where an old man wearing a colourful turban sat on a charpoi. Ravi bent and touched his feet as the man lovingly placed his palm on Ravi's head.

He spoke to his father, and the old man looked up, trying to recognise the visitors.

"Have we met before?" he asked. Ravi and Kumar helped translate the conversation.

"You may know me." Vidya's voice was soft.

The old man adjusted his spectacles and looked at Vidya trying to remember or recognise her.

"I am sorry dear, I have grown old. My memory is fading". His voice was weak and his hands trembled as he spoke.

"I am Vidya. You may not know me well, but I am sure you will remember me." She spoke of that day forever etched in her memory, the day it rained heavily and she lost her brother.

"Yes. Yes, I remember. How could I forget? Was that really you?" He came forward slowly, held Vidya's chin and moved her face from left to right in the light.

"You were so small then. I remember you crying for your brother." He stopped to catch his breath. "It was too bad. God forbid something like that should happen even to an enemy." He paused again.

"What brings you here again?"

It was a painful task and it took time, with Kumar and Ravi trying to interpret the conversation and with the old man struggling to talk.

Vidya explained that she was looking for her mother. She spoke about how she'd been taken to an orphanage by Gangu.

"Gangu, yes, he was a bad man. Very bad." The old man seemed to remember Gangu.

"Do you know where Gangu lives? He may know where my Amma is." There was hope in Vidya's voice as she spoke.

"Gangu is no more. Bad people meet bad ends."

"Oh!" Nothing seemed to be working. Was there no hope after all?

"But your Amma was a very strong woman!"

There was a light in Vidya's eyes again.

"So you met Amma? You know her."

"Yes. She came. She came to the temple after Gangu left you at the orphanage."

Vidya listened eagerly as Ravi's father told her the story, the past that had been buried under lies that she struggled to uncover now. He gasped and paused many times, taking a sip of water now and then. The guests were served sugarcane juice, but it was forgotten.

"She came to me, crying. She was in rags. She pleaded with Gangu to tell her about her children. But Gangu was a rogue. Your Amma came to me, she got to know of her son's death. She was devastated. She told me how Gangu had sold her to one of the rich traders, how she'd been abused and hurt. She was held captive and when she tried to escape, they threatened to harm her children. She was helpless. She wanted her children to be safe. Gangu kept telling her that her children were safe and in his custody. She pleaded with him to let her meet them once, but he would hear nothing of it."

"God! Will the misery in my life ever end?" Vidya wiped her tears as the old man continued.

"She told me she was given little food, and one day, she could bear it no longer. She managed to climb over the walls and escaped one night. She did not know the place, she had to struggle for days to reach the temple, and when she came here, she got to know of the tragedy." There was another long pause.

"She knew that Gangu knew where you were. But there was no way to get anything out of him. She sat on the temple steps every day, praying for her daughter's safety. She was scared that her daughter would be sold into prostitution too, but could do nothing. She went to the police station, but there was no proof against Gangu. No one dared to speak against him. Then your Amma started following Gangu. She came to know of the orphanage. Gangu was furious, he thrashed her and she fainted, but she did not lose courage. She tried speaking to the orphanage staff, but was thrown out. She knew her daughter must have been there. She tried speaking to one of the children. She bribed them with a few candies that I gave her once. She came to know that you'd been sold and taken to a far off land.

"That broke her spirit, finally. She had lost her whole family. She wanted to commit suicide. She would often sit under the tree as a few devotees gave her a alms and food. I saw her misery every day, but could not do much. She knew that her son had breathed his last before my shop. She would come and sit there quietly for hours. She did not disturb my business, nor did she beg. I do not know how but one day she came to know that Gangu was going to sell another girl child. She silently followed him and on the way before Gangu could reach the orphanage to sell the girl to Kamala, she gathered all her strength and attacked Gangu with a big boulder. She crushed his head. She kept on repeating, 'I will not let you spoil any more lives, not anymore, not anymore,' long after he was dead."

Vidya was stunned. There was an eerie silence. No one knew how to react.

"Your Amma was arrested, tried in court where she revealed the details of the orphanage. The orphanage was raided and several children rescued. But she had to serve her sentence. She was released early due to her good conduct. She came to me again one day. She was sick and she looked so much older than she was. She asked me if her daughter had come looking for her when she was gone. She was hopeful that you would return. She used to sit for hours waiting. Slowly, she gave up food, her eyes were dry. She became weak, and one day, we found her dead under that very same tree."

Vidya sobbed inconsolably. "Amma, Amma I have come, I have come in search of you! Amma . . ." She doubled over in pain as she cried as if the agony in her heart would never be eased. For once, Bill was wrong – it can be too late.

Mr. Thomas thanked Ravi and his father as he led Vidya out. Her feet were heavy and she moved slowly.

Back at the hotel, she spoke to Bill. "My Amma was a good woman, she did not betray me," Vidya sobbed as she narrated what she had come to know of her mother. "She was very brave, she fought like the buffalo mother we saw in the wild. I am proud of her, so very proud. So proud to be her daughter."

"Yes, dear, I am proud of you too. You are like your mother, very strong, very brave. Come back home honey, we are waiting for you."

As the plane flew amongst the clouds, Vidya could not help peeping out of the window, hoping to see Amma, Nana, Thaatha and Sai somewhere in the floating palaces of heaven. She knew it was childish, but she could not stop herself. There was a smile on her face and a sense of peace. She held Mr. Thomas's hand gently as he patted hers. She had found herself at last. She had found her family—her whole family. Amma, Nana, Thaatha and Sai included.

Glossary

Nana: Father
Thaatha: Grandfather or any elderly man of the same age
Amma: Mother
Rangoli: Designs and figures over the floor with rice powder, stone colour, flowers and colours
Baawdi: Well
Manjan: Powder used to clean teeth
Charpoi: Cot with wooden frame, woven with ropes
Dhoti: A traditional long loincloth worn by men in India.
Neelkanth – Blue Jay
Peepal: Sacred fig tree
Beedi: Thin Indian cigarettes filled with tobacco in tendu leaves and tied with thread
Jhumkas: Dangling earrings
Kajal: Eyeliner
Daraanti: sickle
Jowar roti: Gluten-free whole-grain Indian bread
Dharmshala: Rest house for travellers or pilgrims
Vada: South Indian crispy fried savoury snack
Idli: A staple diet of South India made by steaming rice and lentil batter
Dosa: A staple diet of South India, pancakes made of rice and lentil batterSambhar: Traditional Indian curry made of lentils, vegetables and spices usually served with rice, idli, dosa etc
Pappu: Lentil curry

Maavdikaai pachchidi: Mango pickle
Perugu: Curds
Pongal: A popular rice dish
Rasam: A traditional Indian soup with tamarind juice, tomatoes and other spices
Nai: Ghee or clarified butter
Vadiaalu: A paste of different lentils ground along with spices and dried in the sun in small quantities to be fried and eaten
Paal payasam: Desert made of beaten rice and milk, garnished with dry fruits
Devi: Goddess
Pallu: Loose end of a saree, usually falling over the shoulder
Masalas: Spices
Aarti: A way of offering prayers in India.
Agarbatti: Incense sticks
Pujas: Prayers
Prasad: Material substance of food which is a religious offering
Diwali, Dusshera and Ganesh Chathurthi: Indian festivals
Shanks: Conch shells
Gotra: Lineage
Nakshatras: term for lunar mansion in Hindu astrology
Mandir: Temple
Lathis: a heavy stick often of bamboo bound with iron used in India as a weapon
Mashals: Light or torch
Sabbal: Crowbar
Bandi: Push cart
Bajjis: A popular street snack
Jalebis: A popular sweet snack
Ice Gola: Crushed ice ball soaked in syrup
Kulfi: A popular frozen dairy dessert
Bindi: A forehead decoration

Thekedar: Contractor

Rakshasa: mythological humanoid being or unrighteous spirit

Poonam: Full moon

Jhula: Swing

Pakora: A fried snack (Fritter)

Ghagra: A traditional long skirt worn by Indian women

Pundit: Learned men

Mantras: A sacred verbal formula repeated in prayer, meditation, incantation; invocation of god

Angithi: Stove

Krupa: Mercy

Netas: Political leaders

Jaijaikar: hailing

Sigree: Small slow burning stove

Asthi: Skeletal remains and ashes

Maisitry: Mason; refers to head contractor in this instance

Surai: A clay pot used to cool drinking water

Dora: Often used to refer to a powerful lord

Gampa: A type of basket made of iron

Shamshaan: Crematorium

Sindoor: Red or orange vermillion applied on forehead by married Hindu women

Phuljharis: A type of fire cracker

Darshan: Sacred sight